THE LITTLE WASHINGTONS
AT SCHOOL

George delivers the torpedo ammunition to his army.

THE LITTLE WASHINGTONS AT SCHOOL

BY

LILLIAN ELIZABETH ROY

AUTHOR OF
THE POLLY BREWSTER BOOKS,
THE GIRL SCOUTS BOOKS, Etc.

ILLUSTRATED

GROSSET & DUNLAP
PUBLISHERS   NEW YORK

Made in the United States of America

CONTENTS

THE
LITTLE WASHINGTONS
AT SCHOOL

CHAPTER ONE

HOW THEY CAME TO GO

"See here, Martha, John says there's a new school about a mile down the road, and I want to see what it's like," whispered George Parke to his sister one day soon after their return from the North, which you doubtless read all about in the third book of the "Little Washington Series."

"Do you mean you'd like to go there for a few days?" asked Martha, with a surprised look, for George had never before signified any desire to apply himself to lessons.

"Oh, no, not exactly attend it, but to go there after the classes are in and peep in at the windows and see if it is the sort of a place where we might have a lot of fun this winter," explained George frankly.

"Then mother won't permit us to go; I can tell you that right now!" declared Martha.

"I didn't suppose she would feel pleased with my plan, but we are not on parole now, you know. We can go anywhere we like until the next punishment limits our play-grounds," returned her brother.

Martha looked dubious at this last suggestion but George gave her little time to raise any objections. He quickly added:

"John's going with me, anyhow, and maybe I'll take Jim along—just because he will tell his mammy if we leave him home, and you know Mammy Jane will run straight to mother with the tale. Then all my fine plans will be spoilt."

"We—ell, if John and Jim go with you, I might as well go too. But I'll say right now—I won't play any Washington War Movies on the school or any children in it! So there!" exclaimed Martha, emphatically.

"Why, of all things! Who ever thought of having fun with the old school? If we act George Washington's Life Story I'll see that we do it in a select circle—not to the public," said George, mightily indignant at his sister's implied threat.

"Humph! You didn't stop to remember your select Circle when we were at the Hotel in New York! But that roof-garden battle was awfully funny, wasn't it, Georgie?" and Martha giggled at the remembrance of that great war-scene between the British and Yanks, as the children played it to the consternation of the hotel guests.

"Um-m! Guess it was! And the fight in Philadelphia—can you remember mother's face when she saw us all covered with mud? Ha, ha, ha!" George laughed uproariously and his sister joined in.

The echo of the laughter reached John who was teaching Jim how to build a suspension bridge over the creek, but all idea of engineering suddenly vanished when the two boys heard their playmates and thought they were having some sport in which they had no part.

"Let's run and see what George is doing?" cried John, and off he started for the summer-house on the Parke's back-lawn.

Jim's little bow legs went after John as fast as the owner could make them travel, and soon both boys were in sight of the arbor where they could see George and Martha rocking back and forth while laughing.

"What is it—what's up now?" called John, as soon as he could be heard.

George looked around and stopped laughing. What did John and Jim mean?

But Martha took advantage of the new-comers' appearance to say: "Are you two going with George and me to the schoolhouse?"

"Oh, is that what you're laughing over? Some new game?" asked John eagerly.

"Of course not! We were only re-membering all the great Revolutionary Battles we fought when we were in New

York and Philadelphia," retorted George.

"Oh," murmured John, deeply disappointed to find there was no new mischief on the board.

"Oh," echoed Jim, his mouth going down at the corners.

"But that doesn't say we *can't* plan some fun," hinted Martha.

"Why, Marth! You just said you wouldn't listen to any fighting with the school," gasped George.

"And I still mean it, but we can play a game some other way, can't we? We'll have to think it all out."

"When do you want to visit there?" asked John.

"Tomorrow or next day. It'd better be tomorrow, John, while our good-behavior freedom is wide-open," replied practical George.

"Then we'd better get our George Washington Book and hunt up some fun," suggested Martha.

"Come on, then," added George, jumping up and starting for the house, followed by his three faithful companions.

In the play-room of the large colonial home where the Parke children lived, the four conspirators found their pictured "Life of Washington" and hastening with it to the summer-house were soon carefully perusing the many thrilling incidents—seeking for a subject that could be nicely turned into one of their play-games.

"I don't suppose we can dress up in any Washington way," ventured Martha, who had never satisfied her longing to wear a curly wig and long sweeping trains to her dress.

"Not if we have to walk a mile to the schoolhouse," returned George.

"My mother said she thought seriously of sending me there this winter. She thinks I'll learn more than by studying with you two under a tutor," said John.

This was a great surprise. Where would be the fun in studying at all if John were not with them to add his ideas to their suggestions for play? Martha and George sat and stared at their playmate for fully a minute in silence.

"I don't see why you two can't go to school, too, 'cause Daddy says children acquire knowledge better where there are a number to compete with. He thinks it will do me good," added John.

"Ah don' see whar Jim's comin' in on dis school-game," sighed the little pickaninny.

"Oh, you'll have to go too, if we go, Jim. There isn't anything to keep you away, you know," said George consolingly.

Jim brightened up like a new penny and said, "Den le's go tomorrer an' see de teacher 'bout beginnin' to oncet."

The three little white playmates exchanged glances for it was plainly seen that Jim thought the planned visit to the schoolhouse on the morrow was for the purpose of applying for tuition.

"If we went to that school this winter, we could have a grand time playing 'Crossing the Delaware' when the stream freezes over," suggested Martha, longingly.

"Oh, yes! I forgot the Creek crosses the road down by Farnley's Farm!" exclaimed George.

"Why don't you coax your father to let you go to that teacher and begin when I do?" said John.

"When will you start lessons?" asked Martha.

"Next Monday. The classes began school yesterday, but the teacher said there wouldn't be much real work done the first week, so I am not losing any lesson."

"Well, that gives us a few days. Now we'll go over there tomorrow and look things over. If we like the teacher and scholars, there won't be much trouble in coaxing mother and father to let us try it. Besides, Old Ephheim won't be our tutor this year, you know, as he went back to Germany just before the armistice was signed," said George.

John looked his amazement at this news, and Martha added, "Yes, we never knew he was a born German until he got a letter ordering him to join his old regiment. Then he told father that he had never taken out his naturalnation papers."

"Ha, ha! That isn't what it's called,

Marth! It's spelled 'n-a-t-u-r-a-l s-a-t-i-o-n papers,'" corrected George.

But the other children never knew that George also spelled the word wrong.

"What time shall we start tomorrow?" asked John.

"Right after we finish our rooms," replied George, for Martha and he had to straighten out their own rooms each morning after breakfast.

"If we go to school down the road, maybe we won't have to do that horrid work every day," suggested Martha, hopefully.

"Why not?" wondered George, although he, too, would be only too glad for an excuse to shirk the tasks.

"Because it will take us half-an-hour to walk there each day, and we never have breakfast until eight, you see. School opens about nine, I s'pose, like all other public schools," returned Martha.

"That's so! Won't that be grand?" exclaimed George.

"Mebbe yoh Marm'll git my mammy to cook brek-fus by seben ebery mornin' 'stead of eight," ventured Jim thoughtfully.

"Oh, you kill-joy!" cried Martha, glaring at the pickaninny.

"That don't worry me," added George, "because Daddy doesn't start for the City 'til eight-thirty, so we won't have breakfast earlier than he wants it."

"Say, all you! Stop figuring on breakfast hours and get down to work about tomorrow," now declared John. "What time shall I meet you at the corner post?" The "corner post" was the great post that divided the boundary lines of the two estates.

"I reckon we ought to leave about nine-thirty. That gives Marth and me time to do our work and get away comfortably," said George.

Martha giggled: "You mean 'get away without mother seeing us,' don't you?"

At this moment the gardener was seen hovering about the summer-house, so George immediately called out: "We're not plotting any new trouble, Mose!"

Mose showed his white teeth in a

broad grin as he replied, "Ah ain't so shore ob dat statement, Mas'er Garge!"

"Well, this time, we're planning about school. You see John, here, is going down to the Country School and we want to go there, too," hurriedly explained Martha.

"De Lawd grant dat yoh-all do go," sighed Mose, earnestly.

"Jim, too!" added George.

"De hull tribe of you'se a thorn in mah flesh," chuckled Mose, casting an anxious eye over the group sitting in the arbor and then glancing about to note if he could see any doubtful arrangements for an immediate cataclysm such as generally befell when the four playmates were so quiet.

Finding that everything seemed unusually peaceful, Mose turned and left the four. The moment he was safely out of hearing, George said: "I just had another thought: s'pose we take our luncheon like I see other school-children who pass the house. They all have dinner-boxes or pails."

"That's a great idea! How will we get the stuff to eat?" said John.

"Jim can always help himself from the big ice-box down in the kitchen pantry, and Marth and I can get the cake or fruit," replied George.

"What yoh want me foh to git?" asked Jim, taking it for granted that he was provider for all from Mammy's domain.

"Well, cold chicken and fresh bread always tastes good at a picnic," suggested Martha. "And there might be cold yams browned in sugar—I like them cold."

"Oh, yes! And get some of Mammy's fresh quince preserve, Jim. She gave mother a dish to taste yesterday and we got a teeny smitch of it. Um-m! But it's good!" added George.

"Ah'll git does an' den addition whateber else what is good en Ah kin git outen de cupboard widdout Mammy ketchin' me," promised Jim, eagerly thinking of the fine picnic he was to go to.

"Now that's all settled we ought to agree about some fun to play about Washington on our walk down the road," said John.

"We said we wouldn't play games on the school-children tomorrow, you know, because the teacher might not let us come in the class at all," warned George.

"But that doesn't mean we can't have fun on the way there," retorted John.

"Let's look over the book and see what we can do," added Martha hastily, to ward off an argument between the two boys.

"Now, here's a good short experience Washington had that will keep us busy from the house to the school," said John, as he pointed to a page in the book. George read aloud as follows:

" 'To Mrs. Martha Custis,
                    "July 20, 1758.
"We have begun our march for the Ohio. A courier is starting for Williamsburg, and I embrace the opportunity to send a few words to one whose life is now inseparable from mine. . . . That an all-powerful Providence may keep us both in safety is the prayer of your ever faithful and affectionate friend.' "

"You skipped the middle part of the letter," instantly Martha reminded her brother.

"Well, it was only softy stuff, you know—it has nothing to do with fighting," said George.

"But it isn't a fight, at all. He only talks of love and prayers," argued John.

"Oh, but the fighting comes in after he starts, you see. This letter is a sort of an introduction to his fun," explained George, turning over a few pages, and beginning to read:

" 'Washington left——' "

Martha here interrupted her brother by saying impatiently: "We played all that early history stuff last Spring. We don't want to repeat history—there's no fun in it. Besides, Lady Washington hasn't a thing to act in that Ohio war."

"Martha's right about playing an old battle over again," added John. "We can just as well find something fresh and fine."

"Well, here then. Pick out a war for yourself," replied George, angrily thrusting the book at Martha and John.

The two failed to take offence at

George's manner, but immediately began to pore over the pages until a suitable selection was found, then John read:

" 'The enemy crossed the Schuylkill by stratagem'—that means the Creek half-way to the school," explained John, looking up, " 'and their manœuvres made it necessary for us to attend to our stores'—by that I mean our lunch, see?"

"Well, all right—go on," demanded George.

" 'The loss of which would have been our ruin. So we attempted a night's march of fourteen miles to surprise them, which we did by reaching their guards before they had notice of our coming.' See how that fits our case—the school children haven't any idea of our visit, so we surprise them while they are at lessons and hide our lunches before they get out at recess to fight us for it."

"Then what happens to us or to the lunches?" asked practical George.

"It says in this account: 'After we had driven the enemy a mile or two, they were in the utmost confusion, and we were upon the point of grasping a victory, when for some unknown cause, our own troops took flight and ran away in great disorder. This was possibly the result of a lack of ammunition on the right wing. After this, we removed to a place many miles up the road to reinforce our division.' I see it all just as plain! Can't you?" concluded John.

"Yes, but I don't see myself running away from the enemy if I have the luncheon safe with me," countered George.

"Let's leave the victory or the defeat of the surprise until tomorrow. Let's first get away and reach the schoolhouse," advised sensible Martha.

"Da'ss what Ah says, too!" added Jim.

So the four Colonial Fighters parted, agreeing to meet at nine-thirty the next day, at the Corner Post.

CHAPTER TWO

THE UNEXPECTED RAID ON THE PANTRY

Early in the morning, while Jinny, the waitress, was giving the finishing touches to the breakfast table, Martha crept into the upstairs pantry to hunt up whatever her willing hands could take for the lunches. She had already secured the glass jar of quince preserves Mammy had given mother a taste of the day previous, and had her arm halfway down in the stone jar that contained cookies, when Mammy herself bustled in.

Martha was speechless with horror, for Mammy seldom came upstairs to attend to anything. Now she was breathless from the climb up the narrow back stairs, and angry to boot.

"Whaf-foh yoh outen bed dis early?" demanded Mammy.

"It's almost eight o'clock," replied

Martha, disengaging her hand from the clutch on the gingersnaps in the jar.

"Udder days we-all hab a jib gittin' Garge an' yoh outen bed atall! Now whaf-foh yoh in dis pantry?"

Mammy stood with shoulders braced back and her large fat arms akimbo as her hands rested upon her ample hips. Her eyes narrowed down with suspicion as Martha backed up against the table that held the quince preserves— that toothsome dessert for the picnic.

"I was just going to help myself to the cookies when you came in," replied Martha, quite honestly. "But what are *you* doing up here in Jinny's place when you ought to be sending up our breakfast? It is eight o'clock—I hear the clock striking."

"Dass jus' hit! I'm lookin' affer dat brekfus, all right! Now what Ah wants to know, am dis! Whar did yoh-all tell Jim to hide hisself away so early?" demanded Mammy.

"We didn't tell Jim nothing! We haven't seen Jim since yesterday afternoon!" retorted Martha, delighted that she could tell the whole truth.

Jinny came into the pantry at this moment, and seemed surprised to find both Martha and Mammy there. Not that it was an unusual matter to find either George or Martha in the pantry the moment she had turned her back, but to find Mammy there when she should have been in the kitchen portended some dire disaster.

"Jinny, did yoh-all see mah pan of raised biskits dis mawnin'?" asked Mammy, the moment the yellow-faced girl came in.

"Yoh biskits! Whaf-foh Ah want-ta see *yoh* raised biskits?" replied Jinny, loftily.

"Ah diden b'lieve yoh did, but Ah was jus' askin' kase Ah smell foul play in dis house so early dis mawnin'! Now see heah, gal! Howcome Marfa down heah befoh brekfus—tell me dat!"

"Marfa, ho'come yoh heah so early?" demanded Jinny.

"Well, you see, it is this way," countered Martha, for she heard George coming softly across the dining-room floor. "I am hungry and the breakfast isn't ready, so I came out to get a hand-

ful of cookies. Then Mammy crept up
and scolded me."

"Dat ain't all, Jinny! Ah baked mah
raised biskits foh brekfus, just lak Ah
allus does, an' de pan bein' red-hot, Ah
sits hit on a table nearby de area-doah
fer to cool. Ah turns to see dat de hom-
iny ain't scorchin' an' den Ah fin's mah
coffee-pot a-bilin' oveh, so Ah has to
tend to all dat. *Den* Ah turns to git
mah pan of biskits, an lo! de debbil is
done run off wid hit!"

Mammy rolled her eyes solemnly at
the last statement for she was very re-
ligious, believing literally in a devil made
up with horns and hoofs instead of looking for him in an evil heart and mind.

"No! Yoh don' say! Mebbe a tramp
got it!" gasped Jinny, delighted that
she could at last discover Mammy in a
short-coming.

"Tramp noffin'! Ah kin bet mah
boots dat Jarge er John wanted somefin'
today fer some goin's on!" snorted
Mammy.

"Well, if it was George or John what
would they steal Jim for? You told

me Jim was gone, too," declared Martha.

"Jim gone!" again gasped Jinny, thrilling deliciously. "Now Ah'm shore a tramp er gipsy come in an' stealed dem biskits, den picked Jim op on de way out and carryed him off to be a body-servant in camp."

Mammy frowned fearfully at the girl who dared suggest such a terrible future for Jim, but the table-bell tinkled just then and Jinny had to run in to see what was wanted at the table.

"Now yoh'll swear dat yoh hain't seed noffin' of mah raised biskits?" threatened Mammy, standing over Martha with one mighty arm upraised—whether for the oath or for a blow Martha could not say. But she quickly chose what to do.

"'Course I kin swear. I don't want your old biscuits for breakfast, anyway. I didn't know you baked any and I never dreamed you lost them! I reckon Jinny knows—it was a tramp."

Jinny rushed out with an order. "Mas'sr Parke say he am late dis mawnin', so hurry his hot bread upstairs, Mammy."

Mammy scoffed: "Hot bread, 'deed! Did yoh-all tell him de place 'fested wid tramps? All de hot bread ennyone gits fer brekfus dis mawnin' is toast made of stale bread!"

And Mammy marched downstairs more ponderously than she came up. Shortly thereafter, Jinny heard the dumb-waiter whistle shrill and she opened the door. Up shot the waiter with a plate of nicely browned toast that looked quite soft and fresh, despite Mammy's predictions.

Martha had managed to secure all the cookies she wanted the moment Jinny ran into the dining-room, so taking the quince preserves and cookies, she ran out of the pantry by the door that led to the entry which was used by delivery men. Out on the side porch, she found George waiting. He had several empty shoe boxes that he had found in the attic.

"Hist! Don't hang around here, Marth! Run right on to the summerhouse with the lunch."

George himself ran on in advance, and Martha soon reached the arbor, quite out of breath. She plumped the glass jar of preserves down upon the bench and then emptied her skirt of the cookies.

"My, this is a nice haul. I wonder what Jim got?" said George, beginning to pack the cookies in one of the boxes.

"Oh, that reminds me! Mammy is *awful* mad!" laughed Martha, then proceeded to tell George about the pantry interview.

"Jim, eh?" hinted George, grinning.

"Sure! But where did he run when he got the pan?" wondered Martha.

"Right heah—unner de floh ob de summeh-house. Did yoh all tink Ah was goin' to chanst gittin' caught wid dem biskits?" squeaked a little voice from under the floor.

George and Martha then rushed over to the "Secret Trap Door" they had cut under a seat one day when it was necessary to help Jim get out from under the same floor. The "Secret Door" as all four of the children named it, happened to be where two wide boards ran short

and had been joined by extra lengths of
lumber. These joints were separated
again and the two short lengths so fixed
that they could be readily taken up or
put down again.

When the "Secret Door" was finished
so not even Mose could see the boards
had been tampered with, the four children tunneled a secret passage under
the entire summer-house, carrying away
the soft earth thus dug out. The débris
was dumped in a hollow in the kitchen
garden, and the fact had never been discovered. Where the tunnel opened out
under the honey-suckle vine a large
square of grassy sod was kept patted
down to hide the spot. Thus, whenever
it was necessary to hide anything
brought from the house for some occa-
sion—like the present case—the tunnel
or trap-door was used. Jim always used
the tunnel as it was safer for him to
squirm in under the vines than be found
in the summer-house by Mose.

Now the two accomplices in crime
assisted Jim up out of the Secret Door
and Jim carefully carried the pan of
raised biscuits with him. Martha

grinned as she wondered what would come upon them should they be found guilty of using the biscuits for luncheon that day, instead of having them for breakfast as Mammy had intended.

"Dat ain't all, neider! Ah'se ben wukkin all de time mah Mammy's ben gittin' brekfus. Ah got out to de icebox an' foun' a hull briled chicken what's foh lunch upstahs, Ah rekon.

"So I wrapt him in a newspaper an' fetched him out fust. Ah lef' him unner de steps of the back stoop while Ah went back to hunt fer moah stuff.

"Ah foun' a bottle of sweet pickles an' a lot of sausages, so Ah tuk dem too. Yoh-all will fin' dem in dat paper. But when Ah smelt dem biskits, Ah jus' coulden hep bringin' 'em fer yoh-all.

"But, lemme tell yoh! It was *some* wok gittin' all dat stuff ober heah widdout habin' dat Mose see me cartin' hit!"

Jim told his story with a pair of eyes constantly rolling back and forth, while his tones rose and fell like a camp meeting song. At regular intervals he syncopated his tale, making his act and escape sound quite thrilling to his two admirers.

"Well, get the paper bundle out, Jim, and I will wrap everything up carefully in a box," said George, removing a lid from an empty box while Jim obediently crawled back into the Secret Tunnel and brought up the chicken and pickles.

"That's a good boy! Now I'll pack everything up," said George, in a voice that was meant to convey the impression that he was about to labor manfully for the others in packing the lunch.

Martha, without saying a word, had meantime packed the raised biscuits in a box and was now tying down the lid with a bit of string she found dangling from a dried Morning-Glory trellis.

"That makes two boxes all ready— one with cookies and one with biscuits," said Martha, placing the boxes next to the quince preserve.

"We'd better not leave them here while we eat breakfast 'cause Mose is sure to find them," said George.

"That's so! We'd better carry them over to the Corner Post and hide them under the hedge," suggested Martha.

"M-a-r-tha!! G-ee-o-rr-ge!!" sounded someone's voice from the back piazza.

"A-l-l—rrr-ighttt-!!" shouted both children, making a megaphone of their hands.

"Co-ome in-to Brr-eak-fas-st!" sounded again.

"Al-l—Rrr-ighttt!!" again replied Martha and George.

"Say, Jim, can't you carry these over there?" asked George.

"Why, it will take him an hour to do it all, and Mose is sure to spy him before he's through! I say we hurry and help him get the things over before we go in to breakfast," advised Martha.

"It's most nine o'clock, I reckon," objected George. "And we wanted to start by half-past."

"Ah'll carry dem ober fer yoh-all. Ah don' want no brekfus' no-how, kase mah Mammy'll put me in bed an' Ah cain't go wid yoh-all," explained Jim.

"Well, you can eat all the breakfast you want the very minute we get out of sight, Jim. But we ain't going to let you get caught with all these goods and

then we won't be able to get away at all
—nine-thirty or no time!" declared
Martha, picking up the box of cookies
and jar of preserves.

Without another word, George
picked up the box of pickles and
chicken, and Jim brought up the rear
carrying the box of biscuits. They
dodged back and forth, from bush to
shrub, until they were safely on the
other side of the wide lawn where the
trees offered a screen from any eyes
peering from the house.

When the lunch boxes were safely
hidden back under the privet hedge, Jim
sauntered over to John's house to meet
him, and incidentally say good-morning
to his daddy, should he happen to meet
him. But George and Martha raced
back to the house to get in to breakfast
before the time when the door closed.
It had been made a cast-iron rule by
father and mother, that any tardy member of the family should be debarred
from entrance to the dining-room once
mother was ready to leave the table.

There were not many seconds to
spare when George and Martha ran in

quite breathless. In fact, mother must have been dallying somewhat with her morning's mail, as her coffee was so cold that she had Jinny bring in a fresh cup when the two delinquents came in.

"What kept you both so late, children?" asked Mrs. Parke.

"Didn't you hear about Mammy and Jim?" asked Martha in feigned surprise.

Mother looked keenly at her daughter. She could always tell when Martha was in earnest. Now she replied: "What has your running about in the garden got to do with the missing biscuits?"

"Oh, I didn't mean the raised biscuits, Mother; I mean that Mammy told me her Jim was missing and she couldn't find him."

"Oh, indeed! Jinny told me the biscuits were missing and that you were in the pantry before breakfast was ready. I thought that perhaps, Jim and the biscuits, coupled with your unusual visit to the pantry, might have been intentional."

Martha watched her mother's face

closely, but there was not a hint of a smile so she wondered how much of the truth mother knew. Wasn't it uncanny how mothers always knew everything —even the most secret plans that no one could have whispered about!

"And then there was George! I never knew him to be up before breakfast in the attic clearing up his scattered toys so industriously as he was this morning," added mother, turning to look at her son.

"Ye-es," sighed George, as if tired from the exertion, "I had to find a box I wanted this morning, and I had to hunt."

"Did you find one? I know where there are several."

"Oh, yes, thank you, mother,—I got one at last," said George, feeling rather small when his mother was so generous.

"What did you propose to do this morning, children?"

"We thought of playing with John. He is going to go to the Country School down the road, you know, beginning next week," said George.

"Yes, and your father thinks it will

be best for both of you to go, too. What do you think of the plan?" asked mother.

George and Martha exchanged looks. Here was exactly what they wanted, but coming from father it was not as alluring as if they had to try hard to win his approval of the idea.

Mother saw and understood at once, but the children did not see that she comprehended the situation. She now added: "It was father's plan, but now that we are speaking of it, I do not think I will approve of it. I have an entirely different idea for your schooling this winter. I shall see how it works out."

"Did you tell father about yours?" asked George, feeling disappointed to find his mother had a different plan from theirs.

"No, not yet. I want to investigate first, then if I am right in my ideas, I shall have mine followed out instead of father's. But one thing you can be told now—my plan will be to have you leave home for your schooling this year."

"Leave home?" gasped both George and Martha, fearfully.

"Yes, as I feel sure you will both be benefited by the association with other children of your own age. I will see that the children are all good and agreeable and not easily led into mischief."

Mother smiled at the last words, and her audience felt reproved. But the shock of leaving home to go to school somewhere outweighed everything else for the time being.

The moment breakfast was done, mother left the two disconcerted children and went up to attend the baby's bath, and George and Martha hurried away to join their accomplices at the Corner Post.

CHAPTER THREE

THE RAID BY THE ENEMY

"Heah dey come!" cried the voice of a little pickaninny hiding behind the Corner Post, when George and Martha were seen hurrying along the road.

"Most time, too!" grumbled John, who had been waiting about for more than half an hour.

"Couldn't help it, John. We've got awful news!" called George, the moment he was in hearing of John's complaint.

"What's the matter—can't you get away this morning?"

"Oh, yes, this is nothing! But think of it! Marth and I are going to be SENT AWAY TO SCHOOL!"

George's voice expressed the awful calamity in his news. Martha looked quite woe-begone for her.

"Gee! You don't mean it!" finally John managed to say.

"All our fun we planned for Washington crossing the Delaware on the Ice, now gone to nothing!" sighed George.

"When you going?" asked John.

"We don't know. Mother isn't saying a thing to us."

"Nor to father, either! That's the queer part of it," added Martha.

"I'll tell you what! I will find out everything from my father. He will be sure to hear about it and tell mother, and I'll get it from both of them and tell you," eagerly said John.

"Ef yoh-all goin' away so soon, all de moah reason foh us to get agoin' and hab a good time today," said Jim, logically. "Spechully as mah fadder er Mose mought come along dis away and ketch us heah wid'dall dis lunch."

"Jim's right. And he hasn't had a smitch to eat this morning, either," said Martha, cheering up visibly, now that there was a hope of sport in the near future.

"That's good advice. Let's not 'cross bridges before we get to them,'" added George.

Then the four friends each took a burden and started off on the way to the schoolhouse. They knew the road well, as it was the one that led direct to the station and postoffice. They trudged for some time in silence, each thinking of the dire blow that would fall and separate them for the winter. But after five minutes of this unusual quiet, Jim piped up.

"Ah reckon it mus' be mos' lunch-time?"

"My goodness! We forgot to give Jim his breakfast," cried Martha, stopping short to look around for a suitable spot.

"Ah see'd dat fallen chestnut tree ober dere an' Ah thought it would mak a good seat foh all us," ventured Jim.

"Just what it will, too. Let's climb over the fence and wait there while Jim eats," said John.

In a few moments more, the four were seated side by side on the old tree-trunk, and George was acting as Master of Ceremonies. He opened the boxes and told Jim to help himself.

But the sight of biscuits and nicely

browned chicken started anew the appetites of the other three as well, so they all decided to have something just to keep Jim company.

When this road-side lunch was finished, it was nearly eleven o'clock, so the boxes were tied again and the four resumed their tramp towards the schoolhouse.

"They have recess at eleven," ventured John.

"We'll get there soon after that, won't we?" said George.

"Yes; I'd rather not let them see us coming, if they are out playing," added John.

"Of course not. We want to surprise the enemy."

Soon after this, the four reached the Creek which was bridged by a pretty rustic bridge, but it had solid pillars underneath, making it staunch enough to resist the spring freshets.

"There's the woods I spoke about, where we can hide our lunch-boxes while we go on to the schoolhouse," said John, pointing towards the woodland that began at the bridge on one side of the road.

"All right, and we'll mark the place some way, so we can run right to the boxes when we have won a victory over our enemy," giggled Martha, all anxious for the fun.

So the boxes were hidden under a group of brookwillows that hung right down to the water's edge, and formed a green curtain all about the trunks. Then the onmarching army of four regained the road and looked forward to the surprise attack. As they marched, George advised his army.

"I suppose the enemy will all be studying when we get there, and maybe the teacher will be at the black-board. We can't afford to waste a bit of ammunition, you know, as we only have a little. So we must make the most noise we can with what I have."

So saying, George carefully emptied his pockets of sundry packages.

"What is it?" eagerly asked three voices about him.

"You'll never guess! 'cause I didn't know it myself until this morning when

I was hunting up in the attic!" chuckled George.

Martha had instantly opened one of the small packages and then exclaimed: "Oh, wonderful! I forgot we had them, too."

"Giant Torpedoes—I'll eat my hat!" gasped John, smiling broadly as he began to understand the fun planned.

"Yep! Martha and I put them away on the Fourth of July, thinking we'd use them some time while playing a big battle, you know. Then we went on that trip to New York and everywhere, and never remembered them again until I found them in a box."

"Is we goin' to shoot dem right in de room?" asked Jim.

"I thought we'd creep up to the windows first, and get a report on the situation of the enemy. When our scouts all come together to report, we'll decide when and where to attack. I'll divide this ammunition with you now, but don't drop any or it will go off and we'll have that much less for the battle!" warned George.

Then the torpedoes were equally divided, seven coming to each one, and one extra to George for bringing them.

"You don't s'pose they are spoilt by being in the attic, do you?" asked John fearfully.

"I'll try this extra one and see," suggested George. So he held it aloft and threw it down forcefully upon a rock.

The explosion it made startled the wild birds in the woods, and caused a flock of crows to squawk loudly. The army laughed gleefully, for the ammunition was a huge success.

Having arrived within twenty paces of the little house that was the center of learning for all the children within ten miles radius, the army stood and looked around suspiciously. No one was in sight, and no vehicle could be seen coming or going along the road that ran past the schoolhouse.

"Now, scouts, creep up and get a line on the camping enemy. Don't let them see you peeping in at the windows, either. Better stand away, somewhat, and look in. I'm going to get over back of that lilac bush and spy, then no one can see me," said George.

The four who composed the Great
American Army of Independence now
separated and each found a position
where the enemy could be watched but
where he or she was hidden. John was
behind the wood-shed, George in the
lilac bushes; Martha stepped inside the
front door and hid in the tiny hallway.
The inner door was partly open so she
could not only see but hear all that was
going on inside.

Jim was the last to find a place, then
seeing the old apple tree that had a
crooked bough hanging over the entrance to the school, he climbed up that
and sat astride the bough, able, by lean-
ing over, to watch the children at their
lessons.

George had said: "When I give the
signal of a cat-call you all must shoot.
Hit the side of the house near the windows the first time. Count sixty and
then follow this broadside by another
round, aiming for the windows so the
torpedoes will crack like a cannon when
they hit the panes of glass."

All three members of the army now
waited anxiously for the General's sig-

nal, and when it did come, four torpedoes were hurled at the side of the
schoolhouse from different angles.

As Martha stood just indoors, she
dropped her torpedo inside the room-
door. The four shots exploded at different times but quite closely after each
other, so that the result was all the army
could hope for. The shot fired by
Martha caused the most panic, as it exploded right behind the teacher who
stood near the door. Not a sign of anyone had given a warning, and when the
torpedoes fell the teacher, as well as the
scholars, were so startled that some
screamed, others jumped, and the
teacher ran crying down the aisle.

Then all was quiet for a time. Not a
scholar knew who the culprit could be.
That it was one of the bad boys there
was no doubt. The teacher managed to
calm herself and demand:

"Which one of you scholars did that?"

Martha stood just outside the door
trying to hold her mouth to choke the
laughter.

"Whoever it was had better stand up
because I am——" At this moment

three terrible cracks sounded on the windows and Martha, having forgotten to count sixty, flung all her remaining torpedoes inside the room and then ran for her life.

The explosions and echoes in the room, and the screams combined to make a veritable pandemonium; then George and John, seeing Martha flee, fired all their ammunition at the house and followed after the first retreating division of the army. Jim being straddled up in the tree, saw the boys get away and thinking the enemy close upon their heels, managed to slide down the knotty trunk, but left strips of his pantaloons clinging to the rough bark.

Just as he reached the ground, one of the big boys ran out to see what all the disturbance was about. Jim, fearing he would be caught, threw his handful of torpedoes at the boy.

The boy dodged them but they fell on the large stone steps before the door, and the crowd of girls and boys that had followed the first boy out, were frightened to bits when the six giant torpedoes exploded under their feet.

The big boy gave chase to Jim who was very fleet-footed in spite of his bent legs, so that the escaping assailant reached his confederates before the advance guard of the enemy could come up.

"Now we must retreat in haste but in good order. Our ammunition is used up and no reinforcements have joined us with fresh rounds of ammunition," shouted George, but the big boy heard.

He was puzzled over the whole affair, but he was determined to find out what these four strangers meant by interrupting class. So he ran on until he reached the bridge. From here he saw the four youngsters disappear in the dense woods and, believing them to belong to the gypsy caravan that was encamped in the other end of those same woods, he gave up the pursuit. When he turned to go back to school, George, who was squatting under the willows watching his pursuer, announced to his army:

"All attempts to capture the brave General Washington and his men proved futile. Having successfully raided the enemy camp, and caused great havoc everywhere, the American Army withdrew in orderly manner to their own camp.

"Although the enemy sent forth its bravest and oldest fighters, they feared to follow and attack the retreating Army, for they feared an ambuscade in the bushes on the banks of the Brandy-wine."

As George paused to think of what more to say, John and Jim watched him with admiration plainly expressed in their faces. What a fine historian George was, to be sure! But Martha laughed outright, then said:

"Oh, George! You've got your two wars mixed together!"

"What do you mean?" demanded George.

"You've mixed the Revolution and the Civil Wars so well that John never knew the difference."

"Maybe I did that on purpose to see if you children knew where I mixed the story," said George, smiling with superiority. "But allow me to conclude my speech to my Army, Madam Washington!"

George stood up and placed his hand inside his coat and the other hand behind his back, as many pictures of Washington are taken, then he said:

"After this gallant attack and glorious victory, my men, we will close the present campaign. The Army needs rest and refreshment and seeing the commissary department not so far down the Creek, where we left it under the Willows, we will now proceed to join it and celebrate our escape without loss or bloodshed."

"Hey—see dere, General! Ah shore done saw someone snoopin' unner dose trees!" cried Jim, jumping up and pointing in the direction of the lunchboxes.

The others also jumped up and ran out from under the screening willows, but no one could be seen.

"You were dreaming, Jim," laughed Martha.

"Naw, Ah wasn't neider. Ah seed a man jus' as shore as Ah'm bawn!" declared Jim, positively.

Just then the army heard the yelping of a dog, and soon after, the animal ran out into the open but a long distance farther down the stream.

"Now, dat dawg b'longs to de man Ah saw. Mebbe he tuk our commissary depahtment, General," said Jim.

The very suggestion caused the entire army to run as fast as the bushes and stones would permit, to anxiously hunt for their valuable larder. Not a sign of it was found, but a plain trail through the tall grass could be seen, which the thief had made after he shouldered the four boxes.

"Gee! Now we've got to fight a real war to win back our property," said John.

"If we only had some of that ammunition left we'd frighten him," added George.

"If he is a tramp with a dog, we'd better not attack too boldly," ventured Martha, "but skirmish around first, and see if we can find a weak spot."

"Yes, and let him eat up all that chicken and quince preserve!" moaned George.

"An' dem raised biskits whaf-foh Ah

mos' done got ketched!" added Jim mournfully.

"Oh dear! I'm awful hungry, too," sighed John.

"Come along, don't let's waste a minute here. We'll go after him—we're four to one!" announced George, throwing out his chest with courage.

"But the dog!" said Martha.

"We'll make friends with the dog and then shoot the tramp," explained George.

"If we only had a real gun!" added John.

"That's what I say! It's so foolish of our folks not to let us have rifles when we really need them for protection," said George, wagging his head approvingly at John for the suggestion.

The four then hurried in the wake of the fleeing enemy who always managed to keep so far in front that they could not see very well who he might be.

CHAPTER FOUR

THE GYPSIES AND THE REAL THIEVES

The American Army had almost come out to the other side of the strip of woods they were passing through, when they lost all track of the man who had the lunches. They hunted in vain for some sign or trail he might have made by broken bushes, downtrodden grass, or other way. But not one thing was found. Even the dog had stopped barking and yelping.

"Here's where two woodland paths cross—which shall we take in following our man?" asked John.

"That one leads to the lake, and that one goes along the back road that leads to our back garden," said Martha, reading from a small sign that was nailed to a pine tree.

"We don't want to go home by the back road, so let us take this path. The man most likely went this way to reach the lake. He expects to sit down there and enjoy his stolen lunch," advised George.

"Ha, ha, ha!" laughed Jim, bending over and slapping his knees.

"What are you laughing at? Give us something funny, too, won't you?" asked John.

"Ah wus wonnerin' ef dat tramp knew he was a-stealin' stolen lunch-boxes. We ain't no better en him, cus we-all stole dat lunch, too!"

"You think that is so funny!" scorned George.

"Shore it am!" laughed Jim again.

"Jim's right—it is funny if you stop to think of it," added Martha, smiling to keep Jim company.

"I've found something funnier than that to laugh at—ha, ha, ha!" exclaimed George, forcing his laughter.

The others looked at him, and John followed the direction of George's gaze. Then both laughed quite naturally. Martha stood in front of Jim, and when she saw the boys look at the little picka-ninny's torn pantaloons, she scowled at them.

"You'll each have to donate a pair of your own breeches to Jim, to make up for these he has torn to strips. His Mammy'll spank him and make him go to bed all day if you don't help him out of the dilemma."

"Ah did it when you-all runned away an' lef' me alone up in dat apple-tree wid de enemy pouring out of de school-room ready to capture me," complained Jim.

"Yes they did, Jim, and I'll see that you get a good pair of George's knickerbockers to keep!" said Martha.

"If you do, I'll give Jinny some of your nice handkerchiefs and, and—lots of other things," threatened George.

Martha smiled wisely, and whispered to Jim: "You just wait and see! Don't worry about these old rags, 'cause I'll get you good ones instead."

Jim smiled for he had every confidence in Martha's promise. But they had been going along the path for some time now, and the two boys in advance must have heard someone, for they stopped and peered through the bushes that grew on the bank at the side of the footpath.

"Did you ever!" gasped John, who was taller because he stood upon a stone and could see better.

"What is it?" asked Martha, eagerly.

"Is it de man wid de lunch-boxes?" added Jim.

"S-sh!" warned George, crouching down and pulling John down also.

"It's a big camp of gypsies. They're all along the shore of the Lake. The horses are tethered quite close to us here."

"Maybe it was a gypsy who stole our boxes," instantly answered Martha.

"That's what it was, John!" abetted George, suddenly realizing the logic of his sister's words.

"Then it's 'good-by' lunch!" said John.

"Ah s'pose dem gypsies is all enjoyin' dat chicken by now!" sighed Jim.

"I'd like to do something to get square with them!" said George vehemently.

"Can't we play George Washington on them and get some satisfaction out of it?" ventured Martha.

"Let's all think hard of something Washington did that we can play on these old gypsies," said George to his army.

"It doesn't have to be a battle that happened after Philadelphia, does it?" asked John.

"No—any old war that will make the gypsies see we won't stand for having our lunch-boxes stolen."

"Then I say—let's remember some raid where horses were stolen. We can easily lead those horses away, and play the raid as Washington's Army did. Gypsies will miss their horses more than we missed our lunch," suggested Martha.

"Gee! That's the idea! We'll get the horses away!" exclaimed the boys in unison.

"I remember some of the happenings at Fort Duquesne," suggested Martha.

"Oh, yes! That was when the Indians raided the settlers' homes, so all the people ran for their lives to the Fort and left whatever valuables they had for the thieves," added George.

"That's it. We'll be the Indians and

these gypsies can be the early settlers," declared John.

"Ah'se heard mah daddy say dat folkses kin be sent to jail foh stealin' hosses," ventured Jim, fearfully.

"But that was for stealing horses—we are only going to lead them over to a better pasture than what they are now eating," said George, quickly.

"That's all. Come along," added John.

Jim seemed to apprehend unpleasant results from the unselfish interest his companions took in seeing that the horses had a better meal than the owners could give them, so he hung back.

"Jim, Washington cheerfully accepted the order to leave his happy home and go all the way over to Fort Duquesne to help the poor settlers, and his men eagerly obeyed everything he told them to do. Now I am Washington, you know, and my men must obey me," said George, thinking it wise to quell at once any refractory soldier in his army.

John nodded approval of this tactic, and Jim shuffled after his superior officers as they crept up to the bushes near the horses.

"Now let me instruct you, my men, in your duties," whispered George, seeing that his three companions were close behind him.

"I'll manage to creep out to that nearest horse and undo the rope that ties him to that stump. I'll lead the animal over here by backing up again to these bushes. Then Martha can lead him along the path by which we came. Next I will untie the second horse and turn him over to John to follow Martha. Keep right on going, John and Marth, until you find a fine green pasture."

"Then I will get a horse for Jim, and last I will lead one, or more, if I can get them." George glanced at his soldiers as he spoke and waited to see if there were any suggestions to improve upon his plans.

"S'pose that dog smells us leading the horses away and runs up to see who we are?" ventured John, suspiciously.

"I guess he ran after the man who stole our boxes," replied Martha, confidently.

"Come along—don't let's lose any more time," urged George, impatiently.

The others agreeing to his plans, he then crept up and managed to lead back one old horse without any sound or sign being given at the camp. Martha soon had the gentle old beast following quietly after her as she hurried along the pathway. Then George crept up again to the other horse and secured that one. John then took the rope and followed along the path already trodden by Washington's first soldier.

But the third horse that George tried to untie from the tree was a young animal and pranced about wildly as a stranger began fussing and tugging at the rope. The other horses threw up their heads and sniffed, and one of them began backing and pulling at his halter. George took alarm at the signs of fright in the animals and, fearing lest they neigh or whinny for their masters, he hurried back to Jim.

"Jim, George Washington was a very careful General and never exposed his men to any danger, so I am not going to get you any wild horse to lead, but we will hurry after John and Martha."

"Ah'se glad ob dat, Garge, 'cause Ah don' like dis hoss bisnis, nohow," sighed Jim, jumping up and scuttling off as fast as he could go.

George had great difficulty in keeping up with his runaway soldier but he dared not call to Jim to stop and wait for him because the gypsies might hear him and give chase.

They soon caught up with Martha and John, and when the four that comprised the army reached the spot where the pathway met the road that ran past the rear of the Graham's and Parke's estates, George called a halt.

The horses began nibbling at the wild grass while the General commanded his men what next to do. But suddenly, John offered a protest to Washington's new orders.

"Why, you said we were going to be the Indians that raided the homesteads of the early settlers! Now you tell us what Washington and his army did at Fort Duquesne, and that we must do so also. We can't be both Indians and

American Army at the same time, can we?"

George had forgotten that they were going to be the Indians for that time, and was silenced for a moment; but only for a moment. He soon explained the situation to his men, especially as they were willing to have such an explanation.

"You see, we had to be Indians before we got the horses, 'cause General Washington would never stoop to such dreadful raids as these Redskins practised. But once the horses were safely out of the Fort and led away from the homesteads, why, then, the American Army could chase them and kill all the Indians and take possession of the horses."

"Then we ought to have a fight right now and kill all the Indians," suggested Martha.

"I'll tell you what we'll do," suggested John, looking down the pathway he had come with his horse but a few minutes before, "I'll still be the Indian, and Martha can, too, but Jim and you be the American Defenders and chase us. If you catch us then we will play we are killed and you must take the animals."

"I'll get up on my horse and ride bareback, so's it will seem more like a chase," said Martha.

"I'll do it, too!" eagerly added John, as this was going to be real fun for him.

"Ah cain't run as fas' as dem hosses travel, an' Ah'll be lef' clean behin'!" objected Jim, watchfully scanning the woods.

"I'll hold your hand, Jim, and keep you up with me. I like John's plan and we can catch them and then we'll ride and they'll have to walk behind in captivity," said George, hopefully.

"Here—one of you boys hold my horse while I climb up on his back," said Martha, offering the rope to George.

"Jim'll hold him while I help you up," suggested her brother.

So the rope was passed on to Jim, and George tried to boost Martha up on the slippery sleek back of Old Dobbin. But she slid down again as often as George lifted her a few feet above the ground, and finally he grew impatient.

"Say, Marth, I can't keep boosting you forever! Can't you get a good hold over his back and pull yourself up a bit?"

"What can I get a hold on? His back's as smooth and slippery as a croquet ball," objected Martha.

"Well, then, you'll have to come over here to this little birch tree and climb up that. We'll take the horse under it and you'll have to drop on his back that way," explained George.

So Martha climbed up the young birch and waited for her steed to be brought to her horse-block. Jim led the docile old horse over through the bushes and George called to his sister:

"Now climb out on the branch and slide off on the horse!"

Martha obediently began to creep out on the slender bough but it bent quickly, as young birches will, and before she could catch hold of the parent-trunk again, she was sliding off—sliding before she could feel assured she would land on the horse's back.

It took but a few seconds for her to leave the faithless birch and land plump upon the horse's neck. But so frightened was she, that she caught hold anywhere for safety.

Her clutch happened to come on the horse's mane and ears, but at the same time, Jim stepped upon a yellow-jackets' nest and brought out the furious bees in a swarm. Why should anyone dare to break into their own private honeycombs?

They flew about in anger and alighted upon anything that offered a place to sting. Not only did Jim find the yellow-jackets unpleasant companions, but Martha and her steed quickly realized how they could sting. Off went the old horse, galloping back for camp as fast as he could cover the uneven woodland road.

George and John, leading their horse, had instantly sought a place of safety as far from the scene of assault as they could reach. From this vantage point of refuge, George shouted to Jim:

"Run after Martha and catch the horse!"

But Jim heard him not. He was too

painfully occupied in dodging and beating off the yellow-jackets. He ran here, then there, but the angry bees followed, believing that he was the sole cause of their interrupted home-life.

Jim's cries and woe finally appealed to the General's humanity, and as the little pickaninny ran past him, he complimented him for his courage and bravery.

"You are a credit to the American Army, Jim. You see, you were bravely going to kill the Indians when another army that was unseen, in ambush, flew at you. Some of those awful sharp-shooters nipped you but didn't manage to kill you. Now you will be given furlough and can go to a hospital to be all mended."

George's praise was sweet to Jim's ears, but the yellow-jackets' daggers had left painful reminders on his legs so the tears ran down his little black cheeks as he whimpered:

"Ah've got to fin' some water and mix up some mud."

"What for?" wondered John.

"To plank over dem stingers. Mud'll take 'em out."

"Then you run to the Creek and tend to your honorable wounds, Jim, whiles I run back to get Martha," ordered George.

Jim then started for the brook while George said to John: "You ride on slowly and we'll catch up with you in no time."

So John drove the horse along the woodland path while George hurried back to catch Martha's runaway horse.

CHAPTER FIVE

HOW GENERAL GEORGE DEFIED THE ENEMY

John had gone slowly along but when the horse reached the end of the woods, and the gables of the Graham house could be seen above the pine-trees, both horse and rider stopped to wait for the rest of the army.

George ran back and found it was apparently much farther to go when one was anxious to find a sister on a runaway horse, than when travelling in the opposite direction. Not a sign of horse or girl could be seen, so he kept on going.

He reached the spot whence the horses had been taken, and by peeping through the bushes, George found the other horses had all been removed. Still no sign of Martha could he find.

He felt distressed because he wondered if gypsies would kidnap so big a

girl as Martha was. And would they
make her work hard as he had heard all
stolen children were made to do?

He pondered this matter very deeply
for a minute and a half, when he determined to face the thieves in their den!
He would demand the release of his sister, or threaten to arrest them.

That he might be taken captive himself, never entered his thoughts—was he
not General Washington?

But even as he decided boldly to demand his sister from the rascals there,
so he began to approach the campers
without leaving the cover of the bushes
and trees until he had almost come upon
the first group of women and children.

George looked quickly about for a
sign of Martha as he slowly left the
screen of bushes and became the center
of attraction of the group nearest him.

George playing General Washington
to his playmates, and George creeping
out from the bushes to ask timidly for
Martha, were different kinds of a boy.
He was not at all sure of his reception
from the gypsies, especially if they had
found out about their horses.

"Good-day," he began.

The women frowned and the children stared at him.

"I came for my sister. She just came here on one of your horses," explained George, politely.

One of the women leaned over from her stool and spoke in a low tone to a girl about ten years of age. Immediately after this, the girl raced off for a group of men at the other end of the camp. George began to fear the worst.

"Did you see my sister just now—she rode an old horse in from those bushes?" repeated George.

One young woman shook her head wonderingly, but the other two women signalled her to mind her own business. Doubtless that was what they told her, as George heard the short command in a queer tongue, and the woman who had shaken her head turned and walked into one of the funny wagons.

George wondered what he had best do when he saw the girl returning with two men following. They soon joined the women where George waited and exchanged a few short sentences in the

queer speech of which George knew
nothing. Then one of the men came
up to him.

"Where foh come you?"

"I want my sister—and I want her
quick!" demanded George, not sure
whether the man asked what he wanted
or where he came from.

"Me no see any seester. Nobuddy
here see her. When she go?"

"She came right here a few minutes
ago—I was right after her," declared
George, growing brave as he found the
man was of a grovelling character.

"No, no! We no see no one. We sit
here all time."

"Now see here!" exclaimed George,
feeling irritated at being so treated;
"she isn't in sight—neither is the horse.
Now she was riding the old horse and
you MUST have caught him and hidden him somewhere about here. She
was on him, so you must have hidden
her, too!"

At the mention of the old horse, the
man quickly asked counsel of his companions. Then he turned again to the
youthful visitor and said:

"We no see the old horse but we go with you to find him."

"Do you think I'm going away from here without Martha?" demanded George, placing his hands in his knickers' pockets and standing defiantly with feet apart, and shoulders back.

The man looked bewildered, and the women chattered anxiously together.

"I stay right here in this camp until you produce my sister and the old horse. I don't care about the old nag much, but she rode him and that's how I know she came here," added George.

The men shrugged their shoulders and moved off, while the women looked askance at the young stranger and then removed their work and lounging to another wagon-spot. George stood still for a few moments, then sauntered to the center wagon, where the men had stopped to communicate the news to someone inside the fine trapped-up vehicle.

Here George continued his investigations for Martha, while she was safely petted in a farm-house a mile farther down the road.

The old horse never stopped at the gypsy camp, but ran on and on along the woodland road until he reached a farm-yard. Here he stopped at the wide gate to neigh over the obstacle that separated him from his old friends, and the farmer in the barn hurried out.

"Wall, wall—ef it ain't Old Slow-Coach back again! Here, come in to to your oats, Slow-Coach," laughed the farmer, as he hurried towards the gate.

But the farmer's wife also heard the whinny and she ran from the house. She saw Martha almost in a collapse upon the old horse's back, but she still clung to his mane and ears.

"Of all things! Where did you come from, child?" called she, as she ran over to help Martha down.

The farmer now came up, but he had not seen the rider before, as he was so near-sighted. Now he, too, gasped as he saw the rider on Old Slow-Coach.

Martha was half-carried into the house and made much of. As she was given a drink of cold milk and the farmer's daughter brought a nice fresh cake, she began to recover her usual spirits.

"Oh! I thought he was going to carry me straight to the gypsy camp where we found him!" sighed Martha.

"Where you found him?" repeated the farmer, amazed.

"Where you found Slow-Coach?" gasped the wife.

Martha's mouth was so full of cake she could not reply, but she nodded her head vigorously. Then when she could speak, she said:

"Yes, we tried to find out where our luncheon was hidden when the gypsy stole it—we saw him running away with it, but all we could get were the horses that were tied right by the bushes where we were."

The farmer and his wife could make no sense of this tale as the man said:

"Why, you must be wrong, my child! Slow-Coach has been out at pasture in the Far-Lot for the last few days."

"When did you see him there last?" asked Martha.

"Last night, when I went to lead the other horse out," replied the farmer, a light suddenly gleaming in his eyes.

"That's what it is, John! They stole

the horses in the night, just as they stole the chickens and the little pigs!" exclaimed his wife.

"By golly! I'll run down to the Far-Lot and see, and if they did that I'll have them all in jail for it!" cried the farmer, running for his hat that always hung back of the kitchen door.

Before he could reach it, however, the telephone rang and Maisie, the daughter, answered it. It was a neighbor speaking.

"Tell your dad I saw his brown mare going along the path from the cross-woods-road towards the Graham place. A saucy boy was riding him, for I said, 'That hoss belongs to Farmer Platt,' and the little rascal laughed: 'Well, he is mine now.' Better get after that kid, as I hear there are gypsies around the country helping themselves to other folkses things."

When Maisie hung up the receiver she called to her father and told him the message, but Martha also heard it.

"Oh, that must have been John on your horse. He and Jim and George are taking it away from the gypsies,"

laughed she, her faintness and fright all
gone by this time.

Then she had to explain how they
came to help themselves to the two
horses. And the three hosts laughed
heartily as they heard how the army
tried to spite the gypsies by hiding their
horses because the gypsies had taken
their nice lunch-boxes. But the joke
was on both would-be horse-thieves, for
now the farmer's two stolen horses were
on a fair road to be returned.

Martha was breathless when she concluded her tale, but she had not said a
word about bombarding the school, for
the farmer might have children there—
and what would he do to her if he knew!

"You hook up the young horse, Dad,
and carry this little girl down to the
place where the mare waits with that
boy. Then you can lead the mare back
home, while you thank the children for
saving your horses from those rascals,"
said his wife.

"But first let me pack some cakes in a
paper and get a bottle of cold milk for
you, little girl. As you've had no lunch,

you and your brothers will be glad to have a bite," added Maisie.

"And I'll telephone the constable to arrest those gypsies."

So Martha was soon perched upon the seat beside the farmer, holding fast to a quart bottle of milk and a dozen cakes.

They went by the road that ran along the lake-side and directly past the gypsy encampment. The young horse had not been exercised for two days so he was full of go. They passed the camp in a flash, so that Martha, curious to see what it looked like from the front, had hardly a glimpse of it. But she thought she heard a plaintive howl as she flew past, and it seemed like her brother's voice that shouted: "Mar-r—tha—! St——t-op!"

Still she knew George would be waiting for her at the end of the woodland road, and soon the farmer stopped where he saw his mare securely tied to a rail-fence. No one was in sight.

Martha looked about, then said: "It's funny that no one is here, but maybe they had to take Jim home. He was

full of the yellow-jackets' stingers, you
know."

The farmer laughed loudly at this,
and then asked: "Where does Jim live?
And by the way, where do you live, little girl? I'm going to tell your father
what a fine lassie he has."

"Oh, better not! Mother and father
know we are fine children, but this time
you'd better not tell them so."

"All the same, I'd like to know your
last name and where you live," insisted
the farmer.

"My name's Martha Parke, and I live
away down the road. You'd never find
it—it's so far away," explained Martha.

The farmer laughed again: "Why, I
sell butter and eggs to the Parkes—that
isn't so far from here. And you're
Martha Parke, are you? Well, well!
I've heard tell of you and your brother,
George Washington! Ha, ha, ha!"

Martha frowned. Why did he laugh
like that?

But the laugh must have reached the
ears of a boy hiding deep in the roadside
bushes, for he crept out now that he
heard the cheerful words and laughter.

It was John, looking dusty and frightened.

"Gee! Martha, I'm glad you're back. I was left all alone with that horse, and when he began to act up I had to jump off and leave him. A man saw him wandering around and so he tied him up to the fence."

The farmer then took over his rightful possession and, having invited the children to visit him at the farm, he drove back. Martha then asked John:

"Where's Jim—and George?"

"Why, George ran after you. He said he was 'fraid the gypsies would kidnap you, so he went to get you away. But I don't know where Jim can be. He was going to the Creek to mix some mud to take the stingers out of his legs."

Martha was in a quandary about George and Jim. She was tired and anxious to get home, but she could not leave the two brave Americans to their unknown fate. So she turned to John.

"Well, we'd better sit down and eat the cake and drink the milk before it goes sour. When the other two join us

—it will be too near supper-time for them to eat, as it will spoil their appetites for supper, you know—we will hurry right home."

John agreed with Martha on this point, so they sat down and were soon enjoying the lovely cake and milk. When the last crumb had disappeared, Jim was seen limping painfully along the dusty road.

"Better throw the bottle over that fence, John, and don't say a word about the cakes, or poor Jim'll feel worse," said Martha, hastily.

John realized the logic of this advice and the milk bottle landed back of the bushes before Jim was aware that his friends were so near. Then his face brightened up with relief.

"Dem yaller-jackets damaged mah laigs so bad dat dey is all swelled fit to bust!" sighed Jim, dropping upon the grass as soon as he reached his companions.

"Oh! look at poor Jim's skinny legs!" exclaimed John.

"They're not skinny now—they're nice and plump, Jim," said Martha, trying to please Jim with praising his appearance.

"Ah don' care what dey look lak—dey ain't feelin' so good as ef dey was befoh dem bees got hol' on dem," wailed Jim.

"Did you see George as you came along?" asked John now.

"Jarge? Hain't he wid yoh-all?" wondered Jim, amazed.

"No, and we fear the gypsies got him to keep for a ransom—you know, how the armies used to do to each other?" said Martha.

"Gee! I never thought of that—a real ransom, eh?" said John, envious of George's privilege.

"Pooh Jarge!" added Jim, forgetting the great honor such a capture would bring upon the captive.

"We were just wondering what to do when you came along," said John.

"Don' tell me to go back wid yoh-all —'cause Ah jus' cain't move, nohow!" exclaimed Jim.

"No, but we were wondering whether we ought to go home and tell the folks," explained Martha.

"Why didn't we tell the farmer to stop at the camp and tell George to meet us here," suddenly suggested John.

"Maybe he will, anyway, 'cause he was going to stop and examine the men who stole his horses. The constable was to meet him there, too, and arrest the rascals," said Martha.

"I hope George won't be arrested with the gypsies," said John, as the thought popped into his mind.

"Even if he was taken, the farmer knows who we are and he knows it was George that got the two horses safely away from the horse-thieves, so the constable won't hold him, you see," said Martha, anxiously scanning the long road that led to the woods.

"I see a little cloud of dust away down there," cried she, after a long silence.

"It's a wagon—going like lightnin', too!" exclaimed John.

Then it came near enough for the children to see that it was a gypsy wagon, and behind it came the other camp-wagons, all being driven as fast as the dusty road would permit.

"For goodness' sake! Hide under

the bushes, boys, or we'll all be kidnapped! The gypsies will be awful
mad at us, you know," exclaimed
Martha, forcing her way through the
bushes.

It took no second invitation for the
boys to obey. They were well back out
of sight when the first vehicle drove
past in its blinding cloud of dust. Then
followed another, and so on, until the
entire band had passed and were out of
sight.

"I reckon we can creep out and look
around now," whispered Martha.

"You wait here, 'cause one can get in
quicker'n three can," advised wise little
John.

He gazed up and down the road well,
before he said: "All safe on the Po-
tomac!"

Martha and Jim crept out, then, and
stood up to stretch their bones. As they
did so, a whoop nearby made them all
jump, and someone laughed heartily.

"Ah thought Ah'd rekernised deses
chillums!" exclaimed Jim's father who
worked on Graham's estate.

"Oh, Daddy! Ah shore is glad to

see yoh! Mah pore laigs is so bad Ah
cain't walk no moh!" now wept Jim,
seeing his father might possibly carry
him in his strong arms.

"Why, honey! What got you lak
dat?" cried Jim's daddy, down on his
knees to examine his pickaninny's sorry-
looking legs.

"Dem yaller-jackets. Ah bruk open
a nes' widdout seein' him," explained
Jim.

"Wall, wall! Yoh daddy shore got to
carry dem laigs home, but yoh-all will
have to walk on yoh haid!" said he,
teasingly. But Jim knew he was saying
that to comfort him in his misery.

"How did you happen to come by
here?" asked John.

"Well, Ah met a man down-road,
what tole me how a boy stole his neighbor's hoss an' had him up here a spell.
When Ah heerd how dat boy looked,
says Ah: 'Dat soun's jus' lak Mas'sr
John—but shore he cain't be up to such
capers, now!'"

The children exchanged glances that
were not lost on Jim's father. The latter continued:

"When the man left, Ah started along to make sure it wasn't John, and when Ah saw dem gypsy-wagins streakin' off lak dey did jus' now, Ah says: 'Dat's who stole dem hosses!'

"Ah heerd from a telerphone call dat Mas'sr Jarge was kidnapped by dem same gypsies, an' ouh good constabule let him go home widdout prisonin' him for helpin' hisself to what hosses dem gypsies had tied up, 'cause a farmer promised to stan' good fer him. So Jarge was sent home by dat back road, an' Ah come along to fin' de remnants of his American Army."

"Ah'se mighty glad yoh did, Daddy!" sighed Jim, as his father carried him in his arms, and the remnant of the Army straggled wearily after their pace-maker, on the road home.

CHAPTER SIX

WHO TOOK THE LUNCH-BOXES?

For a wonder, not a word was said to George and Martha about their being away all day, or about their experience with the gypsy-band. This seemed strange, for usually, when they had such an escapade as that day had witnessed, mother punished them in a way to make them remember it.

It was late afternoon when they entered the house hot, dusty, and hungry —at least George was hungry. But they were met by Jinny who told them to go upstairs and take a bath.

"Where's mother?" asked Martha.

"Havin' compn'y in the pahlor," said Jinny.

So George crept softly up the hallway and peeped to see who the company was. John's mother was there having a good time with mother, but George could not hear a word that was said, as both ladies spoke in very low tones.

"I think it's funny that John's mother should call like this," said Martha, when George told her who was with mother.

"I s'pose she got worried over John's bein' away, and came over to ask mother what to do about it," said George.

"That's just it! Well, let's get washed up before supper," added Martha, without giving another thought to John's mother.

That evening when the family sat down for supper, Martha and George found two slices of dried bread on their plates, and two raised biscuits for each. The others had the regulation meal.

No one passed the two culprits any of the other dishes, so George spoke up: "Aren't we going to have any soup or salad?"

"You will have to eat what you have on your plates, then you can have the next course," said mother, calmly.

Father merely stopped talking long enough to allow mother to answer the children, then he continued without paying further attention to them. Mother seemed deeply interested in his story.

Martha and George ate the hard bread and dry raised biscuits without another word, but they could not understand what it all meant. It was a queer form of punishment, to say the least.

"Now we have finished these. What do we have next?" asked Martha, during a lull in the conversation.

"Jinny, bring on the quince preserves and a cooky each," said mother.

When Jinny brought the quince preserves in a familiar-looking jar, and a shoe-box of cookies, from which she took two cakes, one for each runaway, Martha and George were dumbfounded. The box looked like the one they had taken that morning, but then there must be lots of boxes exactly like the ones they took. But why should Jinny serve the cookies in a box—and why bring in a jar of the preserves without mother saying anything to her?

Mother helped serve the quince and passed a dish to each of them, then placed a cooky beside the dish, and told

Jinny to carry the box and jar back to the pantry.

"Is this all we get for supper? We had no dinner," said George in a voice calculated to make his mother fear they would starve.

"If you are hungry still, I can have Jinny bring in a part of a chicken. I believe you will find some meat on it."

"Chicken! Why, you didn't have chicken," said Martha.

"No, we *couldn't* have chicken. Someone stole our chicken, so we had to order something else," returned mother, innocently.

George wanted to ask: "Then where did you find this one?" but he felt tongue-tied for some reason.

"Jinny, the children say they are still hungry. They may each have some of that chicken that was found in the woods," said mother, when the maid replied to the bell.

Martha and George looked at each other. What queer sort of affair was this, anyway!

The chicken was brought in and it certainly did look familiar. There was the torn place where Jim had helped himself to his breakfast that morning. Oh, how very long ago that seemed to be! Yet it was only that morning.

Jinny served a portion of the chicken to each of the wondering culprits, and they found it was cold, and must have been cooked for some time. It was hard and dry from being in the air. However, they ate it without a word of complaint, and when the quince and cookies had disappeared, they sat perfectly still to wait for father and mother to finish. Generally, they begged to be excused as there was always some mischief to be attended to. But the food that night seemed to have a quieting effect on them.

As father rose to open the door for mother, he said: "I trust we may often have the company of the children to the end of the meals."

"Perhaps we shall if they enjoy their food as they have tonight," replied mother.

George ran away the moment he was out of the dining-room and Martha followed, for she knew he was after information. Out in the pantry he found Jinny clearing away the dishes.

"Say, Jinny! Where did you get that stuff you served us for supper?" demanded he.

"Yoh modder gave hit to me foh yoh-all."

"Where did she get it?" asked Martha.

"How shoul' Ah know dat? She don' tell Jinny ebeything."

Down to the kitchen they went, and there they found Jim mournfully seated, his waist fastened securely to the back of the chair. Dinah was just going to sit down to her supper.

"Dinah, where did you get that stuff you sent us for our supper?" asked both children at once.

"Ah cooked hit, to be shore!"

"You did?" from George, sceptically.

"But when?" from Martha.

"Ah done cookt hit today. by yoh mudder's orders!"

Martha and George winked at each other. "Yes, she cooked it all this morning," whispered Martha to her

brother. Then they turned their attention to Jim.

"What you tied up for?"

"Kase Ah runned away agin," whimpered the pickaninny.

"You did not! Dinah, did you
believe Jim ran away?" demanded
Martha, turning suddenly upon the
cook.

"He shore did! Whad else kin yoh
call hit?"

"Why, we only went to school to see
if we would like it better'n going away
from home. We took Jim along, because he can go to school with us—it is
a public school, you know, down the
road," explained Martha.

George caught the idea from his sister, so he added: "Yes, we were not
sure when school was out so we needed
some lunch in case we were too late to
come home. But someone stole our
box."

Dinah looked doubtful. "Does yoh
modder know dis?"

"How should she, when she hasn't
seen us yet. We intend explaining as

soon as she is free for a moment," replied Martha.

"How-come yoh-all carried so many raised biscuits and dat chicken along?" demanded Dinah, her doubts gaining again.

"Goodness me! That wasn't much for four hungry scholars!" returned George.

"But yoh diden have to be so secret 'bout it all, ef yoh wanted to have lunch foh school, shorely yuh coul' hab had it!" exclaimed Dinah.

"Well, you see, mother said we had to go away to school, and we want to go where Jim goes, so we thought we'd go there and try it before we said anything to anyone about it," said George.

Dinah was not completely convinced of the fact, so she said wisely: "Ah reckon Ah'll wait an' see what comes of dis mess!"

George and Martha had to leave at that, and cast a wistful glance at Jim, who sat disconsolately hunched in the old chair. Once up the area-steps, George whispered to his sister:

"There's something queer about this

whole thing. Now how did they get that chicken and other stuff back? Did those horrid gypsies hand back the lunch-boxes when they were caught?"

"Oh dear! I hope not! I'd hate to think I was eating the food they had stolen and had in camp all afternoon, before giving it back," cried Martha.

"We saw a man running away from that willow-tree with our boxes, and we saw a dog jumping about him. He must have gone directly to the camp as we followed and could not see him on the road anywhere," said George.

Martha made no reply but sat thinking earnestly for a time. "George, you didn't see the face of that man, did you?"

"No, why?"

"Are you sure it was a gypsy? Couldn't it have been a colored man?"

"Oh, it might, but who wants to steal lunch-boxes?"

"You don't s'pose—just for argument, now—that one of the men about the place, take Jim's father, for instance, found us meeting at the Corner Post, and followed, eh?

"When we hid the boxes he might have hidden, too, and waited to see where we went or what we were up to?"

George fixed his eyes on Martha but said not a word.

She continued: "Then when we ran back after the bombardment, he ran off with our lunch-boxes to make us chase him. Then we could have trailed him home, you see."

"But he was gone—we couldn't see hide or hair of him, you know," argued George.

"When he heard us bombard the school with torpedoes, he may have thought we had guns and would fire at him. Or he may have hidden in the bushes when we ran past to the road. We never thought of looking about for the thief, you know. We took for granted that he would run as fast as he could go along the road."

"But you forget that dog! He had a dog, you know."

"Any dog will keep quiet if its master orders it to. He may have commanded it to lie down beside him in the bushes."

George did not want to admit that his judgment might have been at fault that afternoon in the woods, but he could not help wondering how those biscuits and other lunch-stuff got back home.

The children fell asleep that night still questioning how it all could have happened, and the next morning father said:

"Mother and I have decided to have you go to school at once. Yesterday's escapade, as someone told us about it, has made me come to a sudden determination. Martha and you will be ready to leave here and go to school tomorrow—Wednesday. All arrangements are made."

"O-oh, father! We didn't want to go away to school!" cried George, actual tears trying to well up in his eyes.

"O—ooh," wept Martha, not ashamed to cry loudly, the deeper to impress her father's heart.

But he turned away and quickly went into the library. The two children looked at each other in dismay.

"Now we've gone and done it!"

grumbled Martha, her eyes suddenly dry again.

"And John will have all the fun this winter!" added George.

Very little breakfast was enjoyed that morning. Was it because the two felt badly because of the imminent departure, or was it because they were given dry biscuits raised and baked the day before, and some quince preserves, and a portion of cold chicken?

No one seemed to notice that the children ate little, and as soon as they were excused they ran out to find John. He must be told the heart-breaking news at once!

Jim joined them in the summer-house, and John was soon heard coming across the gardens. Before he reached them, he called: "I say! Isn't it horrid! Daddy told me about your going away to school tomorrow!"

Then there was an awful condolence-meeting. All four sat like glooms and talked of the horrid times each one would have when separated from the others. Jim seemed to gloom deepest of all, for he said he would have to live all the rest of his days down in the kitchen-basement with no one to care what became of him!

They played that day, but over all their games there hung a heavy pall of sorrow—sorrow at a parting that was now only a few hours away!

Late that afternoon, when John heard, for the fifth time, the horn blow for him to come home, the three friends parted, Martha and George agreeing to write every day, and John promising to reply and tell them about everything. Jim stood by too sad to offer any word of hope or cheerfulness.

John had gone, and Jim now said a quavering good-by to his two staunch friends and associates in mischief. Martha shook his hand but said nothing, while George said: "We'll see you again in the morning, Jim!"

CHAPTER SEVEN

FIRST DAYS AT SCHOOL

As you may imagine, George and Martha were up early in the morning, to take part in all the bustle of going away to school. Now that the parting with John and Jim was over, they rather liked the novelty of going away all alone and being independent of every one.

"I hope the trunks are packed and ready. I wouldn't want to miss the train, would you?" suggested Martha.

"Oh, father said all arrangements were made, so I s'pose he has the trunks ready, too."

There seemed to be no unusual excitement downstairs because of their going away, and Martha had to remind Jinny twice that George and she would be away a long time.

"Then we-all shore will have peaceful days!" said Jinny.

"Huh! You're a heartless creature!"

snapped Martha, going out of the pantry, but not until she had caught up a handful of vanilla snaps and was hotly pursued by Jinny with a wet towel.

George sat on the door-step waiting, and the moment he heard the scuffle of racing feet across the hall-floor he knew his sister had something good to eat.

"Here, Martha—give it to me, I can run faster than you!"

But Jinny had given up the chase, content to call out: "You kin hab dem —youse goin' away today an' Jinny'll be havin' fine times in her pantry all to herself!"

"Mean thing—to talk like that the very last day we are home," mumbled Martha, but consoling herself with the vanilla snaps.

Breakfast seemed quite a merry meal instead of a sad one such as Martha and George had pictured it would be. Father and mother were quite gay and happy, so they could not feel very broken-hearted about the parting. They never even referred to it during the meal, and when it was over, father said:

"Well, the children leave for school today, eh?"

And mother smiled and nodded a yes. Then he said as he took up his hat from the hall stand:

"Well, children, I sincerely trust you will behave yourselves and not be expelled the first week. Better not tell the teacher that you tried to blow up the schoolhouse down the road."

Now where did he hear of that! Who was there to spy upon them? Martha and George looked earnestly at each other.

"Good-by, children," said father, kissing them as was his usual custom when leaving for the City. But he seemed not to feel very keenly their going away, and he jumped into the auto after kissing mother, without any extra kisses for them. He waved his hand, wafted a kiss for all of them and then was out of sight.

"Are we really going today, mother?" asked Martha, half doubting the fact as her father had acted so natural.

"Yes, the moment Pete brings back the machine. You must run in now

and get your hats on," said mother, going indoors.

"Where are the trunks and things?"
asked George.

"I sent whatever you would need at
school yesterday, so there is nothing for
you to carry excepting a lunch for this
noon for each of you."

"Lunch! Is it so far that we have
to eat luncheon on the way?" queried
both children in chorus. But they were
given no reply.

Martha had found a nice new dress
on the chair by her bed that morning, so
she donned it, believing it to be her
travelling dress. And George had a
clean white linen suit with blue collar
and cuffs to wear; now they found their
hats and hunted about for coats. Usually these articles were anywhere—on
the barn-ridgepole, or up in the attic.
This morning, however, both coats and
hats were found in the natural hanging-
place—the closet.

By the time Pete brought the car back
from the station, mother was ready and
giving orders to Jinny for the time she
was to be absent. Martha and George

heard her say: "And I'll be back in half-an-hour."

"My goodness! Isn't mother going with us?" gasped Martha, looking at her brother.

"She can't be expecting us to travel *all* alone!" said he.

"All ready, children!" cried mother, running out on the piazza as she heard the car stop on the gravelled road.

Jinny came out to grin at them in farewell, but the children felt greatly chagrined to find no other servants were there to wish them good-by. Even Jim had failed to put in his appearance to say his sad farewell that morning.

"All right, Pete. Drive on," said mother, quite as if it was a most natural thing to do—this leaving home for a long absence to attend school.

Mother spoke gaily of the lovely weather, the birds warbling, and the perfume of the flowers, but her audience had no heart for such matters. They going away from home and kin!

They were half-way to the bridge that spanned the Creek where they had met with such unexpected experiences two days before, when the car slowed up somewhat. George leaned out to see why that should be, and saw Jim trudging along the road beside his father.

"Well, of all things! If it isn't Jim!" exclaimed George.

"Then he can say good-by to us! He didn't forget us, after all, George," said Martha, glad to find her black friend had not intentionally neglected to bid them farewell.

"Tell Pete to stop the car, mother, while we shake hands with Jim," said George, but mother was engaged in telling Pete about a bad bit of road near the railroad station that ought to be reported to the County Freeholders.

So the car whisked past Jim and his father, and all the good-bys came from George and Martha, who shouted at Jim and waved their hands frantically for him to recognise them.

Over the bridge they flew and now they were quite near to the little country school where they had bombarded the inmates only a few short hours previous. Could it be, that they were now about to be sent away from such joys

and, in the future, made to sit still and
learn lessons properly as other children
did?

Martha and George exchanged looks
as they both had a picture of the fright
in the school-room when they dropped
the giant torpedoes in and about the
place. Mother was looking at a giant
elm tree and failed to see the smile that
almost broke into a wild laugh as the
two mischief-makers remembered the
raid.

The car was almost opposite the little
schoolhouse now, and Martha and
George leaned over to see if any children were to be seen about. Yes, quite
a group stood talking over some event—
that was clear to understand. But what
ailed Pete—

"Pete, can't you steer the machine?"
cried George, as the driver brought the
car nicely up to the entrance of the little structure.

"What ails him?" demanded Martha,
as she saw Pete lean back in his seat
and fold his hands.

"Nothing that I know of," replied
Mrs. Parke, as she gathered her skirt

together. "Is anything the matter, Pete?"

"No, ma'am—I'se all right! Feelin' mighty pert, dis mawnin', ma'am," said Pete.

"Come, children, we'll go right in and see teacher," said Mrs. Parke, as she stepped from the car.

Martha and George still sat as if turned to stone. What did this all mean? Were they not going away to school?

Finally Jim came along the road and hailed them.

"I'se goin', too! Daddy tol' me about hit las' night an' da's why Ah coul'en come t' say goo-by! Ah was a-comin' mahsef, see!"

"Mother, are we going to stop here?" asked George.

"You are coming to school here, but not to stop, I hope. Of course, there will be many days I fear, when the teacher will have to make you stop in after school as a punishment, but not every day—you surely will be good part of the time."

"But aren't we going away on a train

to live way off?" asked Martha, eagerly.

"I trust not. If you fail to please the teacher here, however, it may be necessary to send you away from home to some boarding-school. But surely you will try to be good at least while you are at school, won't you?"

Just then John came running out of the open door of the school-building, and his mother followed with the young teacher.

Mrs. Parke smiled and greeted the pretty young lady as if she were well acquainted with her. Then she said:

"These are the two new scholars I spoke to you about Monday, Miss Amslie, when the bombardment took place. This is George and this is Martha Parke." As she spoke, she laid a hand on the head of each of the children.

Miss Amslie smiled a welcome, and as her two new pupils courtesied in acknowledgment of the introduction, they wondered: "What was that mother said just now about her being here when the bombardment took place?"

They dared not look at John for information, lest he say or do something to commit all three of them. But the tension was relaxed somewhat, by having Jim's father now step up and say:

"Ah brought Jim as yoh say, Missus!"

"Oh, yes, Miss Amslie, here is another new scholar. This is Jim who lives with Mrs. Parke but whose father lives with us. Jim is as much a member of our families as either of these playmates, so it seems right that he should begin school with them."

Miss Amslie then shook Jim's scrawny little hand and smiled so that he was won completely from that day. At the same time a guilty feeling crept into Jim's soul for had he not planned to throw torpedoes in that very school that was governed by such a sweet angel?

It was not yet time to ring the bell for the school-children to assemble in the room, so Miss Amslie said to the new-comers:

"I am really very glad you did not begin school Monday as we had a dreadful time. Some very naughty children came and threw torpedoes inside and all about the building, so that many of the children were too disturbed to continue their lessons. We think it must have been some dreadful youngsters belonging to a band of gypsies that was encamped by the lakeside. We think so, because some of the older scholars saw them run through the woods and follow the stream that leads up to their camp-grounds."

The new scholars never said a word, nor did they look at each other. Jim's father spoke, however:

"Ah was goin' through dem same woods day befoh yistiddy. Ah saw a dawg hangin' about de Crick, an' feelin' shore he was annoyin' a young beaver what's buildin' a dam down Stream, Ah hid mahself to watch. Shore 'nuff, he was tryin' to ketch dat beaver, but Ah got him 'stead. Ah tied him to a rope Ah had in mah poacket, and was goin' t' lead him off to that gypsy's camp whar he b'longed, when Ah foun' a nest of lunch-boxes tucked under a willow tree.

"It struck me dat some ov dose same raised biskits tas'ed a lot like dose my wife bakes, so I carried dem away. Ah wasn't moh den a hundred yards away when Ah heerd dat bombardment, and Ah run, kase Ah feered some Bolshevists were doomin' dis school!

"Ah runned until Ah reached de back road and den Ah sent dat hound home a-howlin' from a kick Ah gave him, and Ah hurried up to home. But Ah heerd dem vandals a-comin' after me, so Ah hid in de bushes to let dem pass by.

"Ah tell you what, Miss Amslie! Yoh was fertunit not to have dem pesky gypsies about deses parts any longer. Why, dem childrun even coul' steal hosses like any western outlaw! I watched while they got away wid two hosses just as easy! Den Ah took to mah heels an' ran home as fas' as Ah coul' go, carryin' dat luncheon wid me.

"An, will yoh b'lieve me! My wife tol me how a darin' thief took dat same lot of raised biskits right from her table where it was a-coolin' fer Mas'sr Parke's brekfus'. And dat same chicken had been meant for lunch. How dey got all de quince preserves and cookies my wife can't say. But we returned all again to de rightful owners. So I say we ought to be mighty thankful, come dis Thanksgibin', dat dem furrin tramps has been driven out of our country by the sheriff."

George, Martha, John and Jim heard this astounding confession from Jim's father, without adding a word of self-defence, for it seemed that everyone blamed the bombardment and the stealing of the two horses on the gypsies, so George was not anxious to disabuse their minds. But he suspected his mother had an idea of the true marauders, or why should she make them eat that luncheon for meals at home?

One of the big scholars now came up and said to Miss Amslie: "Shall I ring the bell—it is nine o'clock?"

"Yes, please."

Then Mrs. Parke and John's mother said: "We must be going home."

"Won't you step in and visit while we begin our day's work?" said Miss Amslie.

"It would be very interesting to us if you are sure we will not disturb the classes," returned Mrs. Parke.

"Oh, not at all; the scholars like company, and I always like it, too, if they only remain during the devotional exercises," explained Miss Amslie.

So Mrs. Parke, Mrs. Graham, and Jim's Daddy remained to watch the school open its daily session.

George, John, Martha and Jim, being new scholars who had never attended a public school before, were excused from taking part that day. They were greatly interested, however, and George and Martha felt so thankful not to be compelled to leave home, that they vowed they would be models of deportment thereafter.

So passed the first day at school, where the teacher and scholars all seemed like saints to the four culprits who were not quite sure whether Miss Amslie knew who the real bombardiers were.

That Jim's father suspected the truth of that school raid, and the horse stealing, George and Martha were certain, but they dared not ask anyone for fear of admitting the misdeed. Then too, they felt sure mother suspected the truth, for why should they have had raised biscuits, chicken that was hard and dry, and quince preserves in their box of luncheon that first day of school, as a reminder that they were not quite forgiven?

But the second day at school, the lunch boxes held a fine repast, so the four children felt their time of punishment was over.

Thus passed the first few days of school, and the four old companions began to like the daily rush to be on time for the bell-ringing. Jim generally rode with the others in the car, but he sat on the front seat beside Pete, his youngest uncle. And many a candy or choice bit of lunch he was given in exchange for that envied seat—where one could see just how to drive a car.

CHAPTER EIGHT

WASHINGTON'S EXPERIENCES À LA GEORGE

THE weeks glided by swiftly to the children who considered school more like a game than work, and consequently learned whatever lessons were given them much quicker and more thoroughly than if they shirked because it was like work.

Miss Amslie was delighted with the wonderful progress the four children had made in American history. Considering their ages, she thought they were very far advanced in this particular study, but then she had not been told how they had learned about Washington's life.

One day, long remembered, in the latter part of October, Miss Amslie started a plan to read for half an hour every afternoon, from the Life of Washington. A new illustrated book had been sent the school library by Mrs. Parke, and the reading began with much interest expressed by the scholars.

The first chapters of the book were not so absorbing to the four members of the American Army we all know so well, but when the teacher began to read from hitherto unknown incidents and experiences of the great general, then the four playmates began to follow carefully every word and deed.

Miss Amslie had been reading the account of Arnold and André, and everyone was listening to the story of faithlessness.

"In the early part of the month of August when General Washington meditated an attack on New York, he proposed that General Arnold should have command of part in the enterprise. This Arnold declined, alleging that his lameness interfered with his doing his duty. Washington never doubted that this was the true cause of his refusing the post, and so he managed to secure for the man the command of West Point and its dependencies.

"Washington exerted himself to prevent the British from establishing a communication between Canada and New York, and West Point was considered the key of that communication. Hence it was necessary to place in command a man whose zeal and courage and fidelity to the Cause of American Freedom was of the highest order.

"Arnold had been considered a most selfish man in many ways but no one doubted his loyalty to his country, so he was given this place of high trust and confidence. But he, impetuous and desperate, and governed by his passions, secretly determined to abandon and betray the American Cause. He entered into negotiations with the British for that purpose.

"He hated his old associates because they had tried to lead him away from indulgences which they knew would be his undoing and he determined to inflict a deadly wound on these same friends.

"Ambitious and fond of display of his wealth and power, Arnold had entered into privateering and reckless investments to increase his income, but it all had proved unsuccessful, so that he was worse off than before he began to engage in these unworthy trades. His funds were exhausted and the creditors became restive.

"In July he presented heavy account bills against the public but the commissioners rejected them as unfair. Then he appealed to Congress but that body reported that he had been allowed more than he had a right to expect or demand.

"So, furious at this failure to retrieve his fortune, he resolved to increase his wealth by committing the foulest treason, the more so, because he planned and perfected his traitorous act merely to gratify revenge and mad ambition.

"Major André, of the British army, was a young officer of distinguished talents and character. He entered into a correspondence with Mrs. Arnold, on the pretence of selling her millinery. But it ripened into treason on the part of Arnold. For after his appointment to West Point, the correspondence continued under the assumed names of Gustavus and Anderson.

"Then Arnold wished to bring negotiations to a speedy finish, so he sent word to Clinton, whose sloop-of-war was stationed in the North River, near enough to facilitate the exchange of messages then going on, that he wished to have a conference with a confidential agent from the British. The amiable and accomplished André was selected for this rôle.

"On the night of September 21st Arnold sent a boat to the *Vulture* to carry André to the river bank outside of the posts held by the Americans. Here Arnold met him and concluded the negotiations for selling out his self-respect to the British. But the dawn came on before the conclusion of the agreements, and it was impossible for André to return in full daylight to the *Vulture*.

"Arnold then suggested that he be concealed for the day and return to his boat at night. So, without his being aware of the fact that Arnold conducted him within the American lines (the very thing that he had stipulated he should not be made to do if he accepted this errand for Clinton), he spent the day with Arnold and when darkness again fell over the earth, he started to return to his own people.

"But the boatmen refused to carry him down to the *Vulture*, as it had shifted its position during the day, to be out of reach of a cannon that had annoyed it considerably. Hence André found he would have to escape by land.

"He changed his uniform for a common coat, and having procured a horse, under the name of John Anderson and with a passport furnished by Arnold, set out alone on his journey to White Plains, or further if he found it necessary.

"He passed the American guards and posts on the road without being suspected, but Arnold had a scouting party, chiefly militia, between the two outposts of American and British armies, and a member of one of these parties suddenly sprung from a covert and seized the horse's bridle.

"Surprised by this unexpected onset, the Major lost his presence of mind and, mistaking the man for a British partisan, instead of showing his passport as he should have done, he asked permission to proceed as he was a loyal British officer.

"Two other scouts then ran up and André realized his fatal error. He offered the most tempting rewards for his freedom, but they refused to listen to a word. He was conducted to Colonel Jamieson, the officer of the scouting party, and there he said he was John Anderson.

"Rather than disclose his real identity and errand, which would involve Arnold as well, André maintained that he was John Anderson, and no other. He was anxious to warn Arnold of his capture and the consequent risk the American officer ran, so actually sent word to Arnold by Jamieson, by begging the latter officer to call Arnold to witness whether he was a loyal American or a British subject—as his captor had declared the prisoner had confessed when first captured.

"Now Jamieson had suspected Arnold of infidelity to the Cause of Freedom, and, hoping to prove his suspicions true, he had notice of André's capture and detention sent to Arnold.

Several papers in Arnold's hand-writing had been found in André's boot, and with other papers was one exactly showing the map of West Point, with all particulars valuable for the British to know.

"These papers with a letter of explanation, were sent to Washington, but the prisoner had avowed he was no other than Major John André, of the British Army, and not a spy as had been first decided against him.

"Washington was shocked when he read of Arnold's treason, and took prompt measures to protect the post, and to prevent the escape of the traitor. But Arnold had already heard of the capture of André through one of his own outposts, and he hastened to reach the *Vulture* which lay some miles below Verplanck's Point.

"Washington appointed a board of officers of which General Greene was president, and Lafayette, Stuben and other well-tested men were members, to investigate the case of Major André During the time he was under arrest, André made such a favorable impres-

sion upon the Americans, by his be-
havior and honorable actions, that, not-
withstanding his being a prisoner, his
judges treated him with utmost respect
and delicacy.

"André gave a candid recital of the
circumstances that occasioned his un-
fortunate capture, withholding nothing
that regarded his own self, but making
no disclosures that might embarrass
others.

"The apprehension of Major André
had caused a lively sensation in the
British Army, for the young man was a
favorite with all, so a flag of truce was
used to carry correspondence from the
British commander-in-chief to General
Washington in order to plead for André's life.

"But the young man had been found
guilty of being a spy, and was condemned as such. All appeals were in-
effectual, and on October 2nd, André
was condemned to die. On the day before his execution Major André wrote a
letter to Washington requesting that he
be put to death like a soldier and not as
a malefactor. But the board, to whom

this request was referred, did not grant this wish. And so, he was hanged, even amidst the regrets and admiration of the American officers who had grown to like him.

"The name of André lived to show what heights of courage and fidelity to a cause a man's moral character can carry him, and this young British officer's name was esteemed by even his enemies and in spite of the degradation of his having been taken for a spy. He proved who and what he really was after his capture even though the term "spy" had to be taken to the gallows.

"But the name of Arnold must go down in history as that of an infamous traitor who had not even the common decency to protect his messenger from capture when it was learned that the day was too far advanced for André to return to his vessel. And to send him off into a hotbed of scouts posted by himself, and then scurry away to safety himself, when his messenger was taken, shows up the weakness and dishonour lurking in the man."

Miss Amslie concluded her reading

by saying: "I know we are all loyal citizens in this room, and everyone of you would fight for your country, and die for it, if necessary, just as André did. But no one would be an Arnold, would you?"

A loud chorus of "No's" greeted this question, and then the teacher dismissed the class.

It happened that Mrs. Parke was using the automobile that afternoon, to do some shopping in the City, so the children had been asked to walk home when school was over. The four started off quite peaceably and orderly, but George was telling them what *he* would have done to that old Arnold, had he been there.

The big boy who had chased the four bombardiers the day of the raid, had often thought he recognized Jim in the little chap who slid down from the apple-tree, the last one in the get-aways. But not a word or sign had ever slipped out to assure this Bill Jenkins that he was right in his conjectures. Still he was always hoping to trip one or the other of the four up by a shrewd guess.

He was walking behind the four children as they trudged homewards, and secretly trying to hear what they were talking about. He had about decided to turn off at the Bridge and go home, when he heard Martha say:

"If André could have run like Jim did that day of the raid he would have reached the British before those scouts could catch him."

"And if he only had a horse like you rode that day when Slow-Coach ran back to his home, he could have had a fine career all through the Revolution," added John.

They all laughed, and Bill now was sure of these four who paid scant attention to him—he the biggest boy in school.

Having learned all he wished to know just then, he turned off to follow the Creek path to his home, but George happened to hear him cross the dry stubble and, turning quickly, wondered if he had overheard their remarks.

"We don't care if he did hear," said Martha.

"He's only a bully, and the others in

school all like us better than they do him," added John.

"But he has some of the big boys with him who like to tease and bully us little ones," said George, thinking of Jim when he said "us little ones" for he would never have admitted that he was "little."

"Then we have got to show him he can't bully us, by teaching him we have the strong arm," said Martha, speaking of the four as a fighting body often called at home "the strong arm."

"He's a spy, anyway, or he wouldn't have been sneaking along behind us so quietly to hear what we said," declared John.

"That's it! He's a spy and we must punish him as one. We heard what Washington did to spies, and we are his soldiers," said George.

"Shall we go after him now, and arrest him?" eagerly asked John.

"No, we must scout as the Americans did, and take him red-handed with all the papers in his boots," said George.

"When?" Martha wanted to know.

"When he spies again. I must plan

something to catch him. Then we will be the judges and mete out his punishment."

They soon reached home and found no one about to object to their playing that the *Vulture* was anchored in the brook and that Clinton was in Communication with Arnold at West Point. John's side of the creek was West Point, the rock in the stream was the *Vulture*, and the Parke's side of the brook was Verplanck's Point where the cannon was mounted that kept shooting at the vessel.

John was expected to reach the *Vulture* safely, but George and Martha stood on their side of the creek with great clods of earth and pelted him every time he tried to wade over to the rock. Jim was General Clinton, and was seated on the rock trying to help Arnold up when he should have reached that refuge. So Jim was the go-between of the American forces at Verplanck's and Arnold's few men at West Point. Consequently Jim caught most of the soft clods in his back.

Finally, the horn sounded from John's back porch, but he had not yet reached the *Vulture* in safety. He suddenly felt determined therefore, to do this before he went in to wash and dress for supper, or die by the assault of mud.

Martha had quite a store of earth cannon-balls piled up beside her, and she now whispered to George: "He'll make a dash for it, 'cause he has to go home! You use these balls and don't let him get aboard or he'll sail to England and get away from us."

And so it proved. Arnold frantically tried to reach the *Vulture* when he heard the third call from the horn, and having all but reached the rock, caught hold of Jim's out-stretched hands to help him up. Once he was up, the canonading from the American army must cease—that was the rule of the game.

But a great clod of soft dirt fell right on Jim's face, blinding him and causing him to cough and sputter. He let go of John's hands and poor Arnold fell back into the creek. It was only deep enough to completely soak him, and with a wild yell of victory, Martha and George pelted continuously until John was completely disgraced. Jim, too, had suffered from so many mud-balls that there was hardly an inch of his clothing that was not caked. To follow up the great surrender of this notorious traitor, Arnold, George and Martha considered it a little thing to wade into the creek to actually capture him. But John climbed out quickly on his side and managed to get away.

The two triumphant ones then offered to escort Jim safely away from the American shores; by this Jim was supposed to go to the stables and wash every tell-tale bit of dirt from his clothing and head. But he shook his head at that.

"Ah don' want'a wash in dat cold pump-water. An' Ah don' want'a go in and' let Mammy see me!"

"Well, what can you do, then?" asked Martha.

"Ah'll wash heah in de crick," Jim suggested, eying the stream.

"I'll help him, Marth, and you go home and get the towel," said George, for he understood why Jim had no desire to go near the barn. His uncle and grandfather would surely be there about this hour.

So all signs of the battle of Verplanck's Point were washed from Jim, and George escorted him to the area steps in honor and a sense of having accomplished much good that afternoon.

When school was out the following day, George asked Bill Jenkins to join them on the walk to the Bridge. Bill was surprised, for he had never been included in this little quartette before. Had he known that he was to play the part of Major André, what would he have done?

They reached the Bridge without any hint of a spy being in their midst, but once the school was out of sight, George said:

"We are going to play a Washington game—want to play with us, Bill?"

"All right," returned Bill.

"Well, you be André and we'll be the scouts who catch you. Then I'll be Jamieson who tries and condemns you to die," explained George, while the others surrounded the British soldier.

"I don't want'a be André!" declared Bill, suspecting a plot.

"But you have to be. We are all Americans, you see," said George.

"I never said I would play such a crazy game," added Bill.

"You said you would, and now you have to play it out," retorted George.

Bill then grew belligerent and doubled up his fists. He sneered at the others and said: "Huh! I'll knock down the first one that comes near my fist!"

But George had trained his army well, for when he gave the signal, all four fell upon the spy and he thrust out his big fist in vain; it fell here and there upon an unprotected back or shoulder, but that only made the American forces more determined to take André to the judge, a bound prisoner.

Bill was soon overpowered, for he had no weak antagonist as he had thought, and now George produced a length of rope with which he bound the prisoner securely. They then marched him off, singing the song of victory as they marched.

"Where shall we hold the trial?" asked John.

"In our vessel, the *Vulture*," suggested Jim.

"Oh, no! Not in a British boat. We will condemn him to die without going to any place. When we get to that old apple-tree near the Corner Posts, we will try him," said Martha.

"Yes, that is an easy tree to climb and hoist him," added George.

"Is the rope strong enough?" questioned John.

"Sure! It'll hang a man, and Bill isn't that yet."

"Say! You ain't going to really hang me, are you?" cried Bill now, in abject fear.

"Sure we are! Didn't the Americans hang André? You are a spy—we saw you skulking behind us every time you got a chance. And you tried to hear us say things, so we just fooled you one afternoon by letting you think you over-heard what we said. Then you had to run and tell it to your other bully-friends. So now we are going to hang you for being a spy." George rendered this verdict in all earnestness and the bully believed his doom was sealed. He began to cry and beg off, but the rope remained taut and he had to go on or have his head badly pulled.

When they came to the gnarled apple-tree with such fine stout limbs for climbing upon and hanging things therefrom, John quickly scrambled up, showing he was accustomed to doing it.

"Now find a spot where the rope will dangle free," said George.

Bill again cried and fell upon his knees begging for his life, when the Parke automobile sped up. Bill was kneeling in the road so Pete had to stop the machine.

"Now what yoh-all up ter?" demanded he, gazing wildly at the rope tied about the bully's neck, and John sitting astride a bough in the tree.

"Going to hang the British Spy," said George, frankly.

Pete sprang out of the car, and caught hold of the noose-end of the rope. "Hang nuttin ef Ah knows hit!" he shouted.

"That's just it. We're going to hang

nothin'—Bill is a bully, and they aren't anything, you know," laughed Martha.

Pete soon had the completely subjugated Bill free and then he said: "Go home an' don' play games wid dese Washertons agin. Kase dey are shore to bust yer haid open ef yoh ever does ennyting what displeases dem."

Bill took to his heels and never stopped running until he had jumped the Creek, and Pete turned to the American Army.

"Now tell de truf! What does yoh mean by dis foolin'?"

"Well, we'll tell you, Pete, seein' how you are all right! That Bill is an awful bully at school, and he tried to make some other big boys play tricks on Jim, 'cause he said Jim was the boy what fired the bombs in the school that day. So we knew the time had come, Pete, when we must fight and get him or he would get us. So we got him, see?" explained George.

"And, Pete, he cried like a baby— oh, you should have heard him promise us everything he had to let him go home," added John.

"But, Pete, he won't try his game on us again! He's 'fraid of us, now!" laughed Martha.

And Jim added with a giggle: "We-all was onny playin' we'd hang him fer a spy—but he diden know we-all was playin'!"

CHAPTER NINE

ANOTHER CHAPTER FROM WASHINGTON'S
LIFE

The following week, Miss Amslie read again from the book that proved so inspiring to the four members of the Army. This time it was all about the closing incidents of the war, and proved very interesting.

" 'It was learned that Cornwallis feared the necessity of a surrender and so had made a bold attempt to escape with part of his army, into the country, leaving the sick and all baggage behind. If he succeeded in crossing to Gloucester, he would destroy the French Legion and other troops, and then mount his infantry on their horses to enable him to push on his way to New York.

" 'Boats were secretly prepared, arrangements made, and a large proportion of the troops were already embarked, and some were landed on Gloucester Point, when a most violent storm of wind and rain blew up. The boats with the crews of troops were driven down the river, and it was not till the next day that these troops could return to the garrison at York.

" 'General Washington now sent terms of capitulation to Cornwallis, allowing him two hours to comply. There being no other alternative, Cornwallis had to consent to arbitrate. But he tried hard to obtain all favorable concessions. He asked that his troops might return home to England, but it was refused. Then, too, he was anxious to secure from punishment any American who had turned to or served under the royal banner of England. But this, too, was refused.

" 'But the officers and soldiers were allowed to retain their private property, and such officers as were not required to remain with the troops were permitted to return to Europe, or reside in any part of America not in possession of British troops.

" 'The capture of Cornwallis and his

army raised a shout of joy and triumph throughout America, and General Washington felt the importance of the conquest he had achieved. He thanked his troops for their bravery and great sacrifice of all things.

" 'The capture of Cornwallis was the decisive event of the war, and thereafter the engagements became desultory and devoid of spirit. They actually were of little public benefit or loss. But the surrender of the British general produced a great change in America, and gave a more cheering aspect to the affairs of the Union. A new impulse was given to the public mind, and the ray of peace seemed now to burst through the gloom of battle and promise plenty for the future.

" 'So in England when Parliament met and debated on ending or continuing the war in America, it was voted to end the strife. But there were many unhappy and annoying incidents continued for a time after it became known that the strife was at an end, and these wretched deeds kept Washington wor-

ried and occupied in seeing that justice
was done to all concerned."

"So, now, children, this will end the
reading of the fight for American Freedom, but I propose reading each day
from the private life of Washington as
a farmer, also of his life as President
of this Country. The classes are dismissed for the day."

No sooner were the four playmates
on the way home, than George exclaimed: "My, but we'll have fun
playing Cornwallis, won't we?"

"On our crick to home?" asked Jim,
eagerly.

"No, that is too small to have some
kinds of boats on it. You see, we have
to let the storm drive us away from
Gloucester, where we want to land.
Now I was thinking of using the big
Creek down by the Bridge."

"But we haven't any boats, George,"
demurred John.

"Build some, then. Cornwallis didn't
have any either when he started out,
but he managed to get some; that is
what we must do."

"Not real boats, George!" exclaimed Martha.

"I don't know what they'll be, but they'll ride the water. I'm going to think it all out and we'll play it on Saturday when there aren't any children around the school to bother us."

"Then we can play the school is New York, where we are going to march to when we land," suggested John.

"Well, Cornwallis never needed New York, and so won't we, if we play we're his army. But we can make believe that it is there, if you want to."

Friday afternoon passed and still George gave no sign of having found the boats, or of thinking of a substitute for them. John hinted several times, that he would be relieved to know what Cornwallis planned to do the following day, but the General seemed greatly bothered and paid no attention to his army.

Saturday morning the four met at the Corner Post as had been agreed upon, and still no word of boats, nor sign of anything other than George having a hammer and a box of nails.

"Well, Cornwallis is ready—are you?" asked he.

At that, the three faces smiled and John heaved a sigh, for he had feared lest their fun be ruined by the lack of boats.

"Ah brung some dinneh," ventured Jim, producing a paper bag of odds and ends.

"Good! The army must eat if it has to fight," said George.

"And I filled my pockets with ginger-snaps," added Martha, displaying the bulging pockets which were pinned at the top with huge safety-pins.

"I didn't know you'd bring anything, so I took all the apples I could carry," now said John, patting the front of his blouse which was certainly protruding like a fat man's front.

"Better and better! We won't have to reach New York to get food, then," laughed George.

The four members of Cornwallis's army trudged along the road, planning eagerly how they would sail to Gloucester, but soon George said:

"Somehow I feel hungry. Suppose we have some ginger-snaps."

"I was thinking they looked mighty good!" added John.

"One a-piece around—no more!" declared Martha, unpinning a pocket and carefully removing four snaps.

When the last crumb was gone, Jim smacked his lips.

"Um-m! Hit taks mah mammy to bake ginger-snaps!"

The others laughed, and John added: "Just for that, we ought to have another one to see if Jim is right."

Martha frowned but there were three votes to one, so she had to consent to giving out another snap to each one.

"Now, not another one, even if you cry for it!" said she.

Finally they reached the Bridge, but no boats or material were in sight. George smiled knowingly, however, and continued his walk across the Bridge.

The others followed, and George kept on until he reached the schoolhouse.

"You said we wouldn't need the

school, and here you are the very first thing!" exclaimed Martha.

"When I said that, I didn't know that boats were so scarce. Now we have to get them from New York, if we want to fight to-day."

Still he had not explained where he would be able to secure boats, so the three members of the common army followed the general to the wood-shed.

"See this shed-door? Well, there is only one hinge left and that I can remove very easily. Then Jim and John will carry it to the Creek for one boat. I found several nice boards up on the beams, and I'm going to nail them together for the other boat. Martha, you can help me pull the boards down," explained George.

The boys worked at the single hinge until the screws were pulled from the old wooden frame of the door, and then they had a boat. If one could close the seeing-eyes and try to see a boat with the mind's eye, one could have a wonderful steamer, or any sort of vessel needed for this enterprise. That is what Cornwallis's army did in this instance,

John and Jim never thought of objecting to doing the heaviest work while George remained at the shed to nail some boards into a raft. But, you see, Cornwallis was a general, while his army had to obey and do the hard work.

There was many a sigh and rest before John and Jim had finished the work of carrying the boat to the Creek, but when they finally returned to the woodshed, they were delighted to find that George, with Martha's help, had nailed three boards together and had produced another fine vessel. One could see the Union Jack flying from the mast-heads if one had any kind of an imagination.

This second boat was also carried to the stream by John and Jim, while George dragged an extra board and Martha carried several short lengths of timber, in case the vessel needed repairs. George did not explain to his admiring army that the nails he had were only a half-inch longer than the thickness of the planks, so the cross-boards were not as securely nailed in as might be expected from the looks of the construction.

The two vessels were launched amidst the hurrahs of the English Army, and then George said: "As General, I must board the flag-ship, you know. I am going to tie my red scarf on a stick and fasten the stick in the key-hole of the wood-shed door."

This was done even as he explained, and then the General climbed over on the old door. He looked about for part of the army to follow him on board, but it was unwise to choose. So he said:

"You three will have to draw lots to see who comes on with me."

Three blades of grass were the lots that would determine the fate of such an important matter. Martha drew the longest blade and was the favored one.

Then John and Jim managed to balance themselves while they got on the three-board-boat, and George gave the signal to start for Gloucester.

He managed to pole off from the bank without any difficulty for the shed-door was heavy and well-cross-planked. Also it was wide enough to float smoothly. But the three-plank-boat George had built for Jim and John was con-

structed of different thicknesses of
wood, and the weight was unevenly
balanced. Consequently the raft would
not float as it should.

There was quite a strong current
flowing under the Bridge, and once
George poled out into it, his shed-door
was drawn along until it travelled won-
derfully without poling or work from
the General.

"Hey there! See how we are sailing!
I tell you what, we can play the storm
caught us right off. Maybe we will
land on the Long Island shore, who
knows?"

"Gee! I wish this old sail-boat would
go like yours!" grumbled John, driving his pole hard against a rock on the
shore.

Now it happened that Jim also
pushed hard against the bank at the
same time, and the two boys standing
on the middle plank, which was the
thickest of the three, failed to note how
the under-pieces were coming loose. As
they pushed together against the inflow-
ing current from the middle of the
stream, the board nearest the shore came

loose completely and floated away on the face of the water.

"Oh! Our ship's sinking!" cried John, frantically.

"Jarge! Jarge—Ah means General Cohnwalls! Help save us!" shrieked Jim, forgetting to pole and thus permitting the two-plank-boat to swing around and hit the shore with a hard bump.

Before George could carefully turn about to see what the trouble could be with his other vessel, Jim had been thrown over and was half in the water and half on the board.

John knew he must save his crew, so he dropped his pole and laid flat out to pull Jim on board again. But the extra weight on the heavy plank caused it to tilt and roll both boys in the Creek.

George and Martha saw the accident but their shed-door vessel was sailing so swiftly on the current of the Creek that they could not stop, nor could they even guide it. It went as it was enticed by the current.

"Try to wade out and we'll run in

down on the sand-banks and come back
to help!" shouted George.

John could swim a little, but Jim was
afraid to try, so he was helpless.

"Can't you touch bottom with your
feet?" asked John, who was splashing
about wildly, thinking he was swimming.

"Ah'se got mah feets on a big flat
stone, but Ah ain't goin' to step off to
try and see ef Ah kin tech bottom!" declared Jim, with a touch of independence most unusual for him.

"No, no—don't try! Just stand as
still as you can on that rock while I
swim out and help you with a pole," advised John.

But John floundered and floundered
about without finding himself much
nearer the bank. He had managed to
keep his head above water, and that was
about all.

CHAPTER TEN

THE RESCUE

"Ah says it's mighty cold standin' in this water lak dis, John," whimpered Jim, after several minutes of patient waiting for his friend to swim ashore and help him out.

"Just a minute more—I'll get there!" gasped John, breathlessly, as he tried to get a hold on an over-hanging bush.

Perhaps he would have actually landed himself, but it would have taken more than a minute. However, he was not put to the test, as Pete drove up just then, having gone to the station to meet some week-end visitors for Mrs. Parke. They had not come on that train and Pete was leisurely driving back.

He heard the shouting from the Creek and wondered what could have happened. As he drove the car out from the screen of trees and bushes that grew along the roadside near the

Bridge, he saw the two boys in the water. Not stopping to question how they got there, he jumped from the car, and in a few great leaps was clutching John's wet hands.

It took but a moment to land John, and then he turned to rescue Jim. But his nephew was too far out on the stone to reach from the shore, so Pete encouraged him by saying:

"Now in just a minute Pete's shoes'll be off an' his coat and trousers!"

As he spoke Pete hastily unlaced his chauffeur's leggings and boots and threw off his coat. He did not stop to remove any other clothing because Jim cried pitifully:

"O-oo! Ah'se shibberin' lak de ague!"

Pete jumped in and in a jiffy had little Jim up and out. Then he began scolding like a young uncle can.

"Whaffoh yoh git in dat scrape? Don' you know no better'n t' leave home to play down in dis crick! Dis crick runs fas'er an' fas'er till it gits to de saw-mill, an' den it tumbles down unner dat wheel, where yoh-all would git crushed like flour!"

"Oh, Pete! Then Martha and George will come out of that mill all in little powder-bits, won't they?" howled John fearfully.

"Jarge and Marta? Whey am dey?" cried Pete, aghast.

"Their boat sailed out to the middle and away they went. If they couldn't land on the sand-flats they are going over the falls by this time!" John had a vivid imagination, you see.

Pete groaned but hurriedly threw on his coat. Turning to the other two, he commanded sternly: "Yoh two start and run home just as fas' as yoh kin. Run as fas', Ah say, as yoh kin so as to warm up yohr blood to keep from ketchin' cold. Ah'm goin' to drive lak mad to ketch dem bad chilluns from goin' over on dat wheel."

The shoes were flung in the car and Pete went in after them. Then he rushed off with a roar, and a cloud of gasoline-smoke. The two soaked and shivering remnants of Cornwallis's army began to run for home as they had been told to do, and soon reached John's house where he advised Jim to stop and dry himself.

Jim knew what awaited him if his mammy saw him in such a state, so he meekly followed John's suggestion and the two stole up the back-stairs to find Amanda, who would help them without telling anyone.

George and Martha thoroughly enjoyed the lively trip on the current of the Creek, but they had never heard of the grist-mill, which, to tell the truth, was several miles from the Bridge.

Martha felt a deep concern about the fate of the other half of the army, but George encouraged her by saying:

"Oh, they'll manage to get out, don't worry!"

"We're almost at the sand-flats," said Martha, after another short silence.

"I'd like to sail on as this is fine!" suggested George.

"No, you won't! We said we'd jump off and run back to save them, and so we will."

"Do you want to go alone?" ventured George.

"Cornwallis, you aren't going to get out of helping save your army just because you want to enjoy this trip? This isn't a pleasure trip, anyway—you forget yourself! This is a sad business of trying to reach Gloucester."

Martha used the strongest argument she could—without being aware of it—by appealing to the General in George. So he got upon his knees to watch for the flats which were shallow places on one side of the stream.

"There they are—down on the right-hand side. Now you try to jump when we get near, and I will drive the pole into the sand to hold the ship."

George managed to get upon his feet and held the pole ready to drive down as they neared the sand-flats. They were just grazing the upper edge of the first little mound of sand when Martha jumped clear and landed upon dry sand. But the impetus given the raft as she jumped sent it out into midstream again.

Before George could drive the pole in to anchor the raft, he was being carried along again on the swift current.

"Jump, George, and swim to shore!" shouted Martha.

"No, you go back and help the others while I try to land down by the back-road," called George.

He was soon out of sight around a bend in the stream, so Martha had to walk back alone to help her confeder-ates. The bushes and briars were brit-tle and would get caught in her skirt and stockings, so she presented a ragged appearance when she finally emerged on the road. But there was no sign of John or Jim at the Bridge when she got there.

She examined the ground for possible tracks, and found a pair of large-sized socks on the bank. She was sure they were not Jim's or John's! Then she found great spotches of mud where feet had stamped water into the soil, and these tracks led up to the Bridge. Here she found automobile tire-tracks, and a trail made by four feet crossing the Bridge. These she was sure belonged to John and Jim, so she followed them home.

George felt no fear, for he had no

knowledge of a grist-mill being several miles farther down the Creek, but when he got near the cross-road that ran at the rear of his home-estate, he managed to coax the raft over to the shore, and as his vessel gradually floated out of the power of the current, he soon had it safely driven into the soft bank.

He climbed up the steep bank and gained the old wooden bridge that spanned the stream, just as Pete drove madly up on his way to rescue Martha and George from the mill-wheel.

"Hello, Pete! Where you speeding to?" called George.

Pete glared at him but did not reply. He threw open the door and motioned George to get in. Then he managed to ask:

"Where's Martha?"

"Home, I reckon, by this time."

Pete then drove home but not a word was exchanged between the two. Pete stopped the car at the garage and merely motioned George to walk to the house.

There the General found the Martha side of his army waiting anxiously for

news from him, but Jim and John were
not to be seen.

"I bet they are over at John's," said
George.

And there they found the two that
made up the other half of the British
Army, enjoying a huge slice of ginger-
bread.

"I'm never going to play British
again!" declared John.

"Why?" asked George.

" 'Cause something always happens
when we are British. Washington's
Army is good enough for me!"

"Well, you know what Teacher
said in school yesterday—Washington's fighting days were over and she
was going to read how he lived on a
farm. Then she was going to read
about his life as President," said
Martha.

"I think we will have heaps of fun
playing farmer," said George.

"And it won't be half so dangerous,"
added John, thinking of his recent
swimming test.

"Oh, we'll find plenty of exciting

things to play. I can think of several right now," replied George.

"Don't try to remember any now, George, 'cause I want Amanda to get us some ginger-bread," whispered Martha.

That silenced George, and soon all four were munching extra slices of hot ginger-bread.

When the long idle days of the summer vacation came, there were more plays from the life of Washington. Martha asserted her rights, George kept his promise, and they all discovered new thrills. How this was accomplished is told in "The Little Washingtons' Holidays."

THE END